'There's a picture of Maria, God and me. There. The *black* poodle, that's me!'

Helmut Krausser

The Great Bagarozy

Translated by
Mike Mitchell

Dedalus

Funded by
THE
ARTS
COUNCIL
OF ENGLAND

Dedalus would like to thank Inter Nationes in Bonn and The Arts Council of England in London for subsidizing the publication of this book

> supported by
> Inter Nationes – Bonn

Published in the UK by Dedalus Ltd, Langford Lodge, St Judith's Lane, Sawtry, Cambs, PE17 5XE

ISBN 1 873982 04 6

Distributed in the United States by Subterranean Company, P.O. Box 160, 265 South Fifth Street, Monroe, Oregon 97456

Distributed in Australia & New Zealand by Peribo Pty Ltd, 58 Beaumont Road, Mount Kuring-gai, N.S.W. 2080

Distributed in Canada by Marginal Distribution, Unit 102, 277 George Street North, Peterborough, Ontario, KJ9 3G9

Originally published under the title Der Grosse Bagarozy
Copyright © 1997 by Rowohlt Verlag Gmbh, Reinbek bei Hamburg
Translation copyright © Mike Mitchell 1998

Typeset by RefineCatch Ltd, Bungay, Suffolk
Printed in Finland by Wsoy

A C.I.P. listing for this book is available on request.

THE AUTHOR

Helmut Krausser was born in Esslingen in 1964. He studied archaeology, history of art and theatre in Munich from 1985 to 1989, while working intermittently as a night-watchman, pop singer, radio announcer and journalist. His plays for the theatre have been performed throughout Germany and abroad. He is the author of five novels and two collections of short stories.

THE TRANSLATOR

Mike Mitchell is one of Dedalus's editorial directors and is responsible for the Dedalus translation programme.

His publications include *The Dedalus Book of Austrian Fantasy: the Meyrink Years 1890/1932*; *Harrap's German Grammar* and a study of Peter Hacks.

Mike Mitchell's translations include *The Road to Solitude* by Paul Leppin and the novels of Herbert Rosendorfer and Gustav Meyrink.

Mike Mitchell won the T.L.S. Schlegel-Tieck German Translation Prize in 1998 for *Letters Back to Ancient China* by Herbert Rosendorfer.

His current projects include a new translation of the 17th century classic *Simplicissimus* by Grimmelshausen.

Contemporary Literature from Dedalus

The Experience of the Night – Marcel Béalu £8.99
Primordial Soup – Christine de la Monica £8.99
Music, in a Foreign Language – Andrew Crumey £7.99
D'Alembert's Principle – Andrew Crumey £7.99
Pfitz – Andrew Crumey £7.99
The Acts of the Apostates – Geoffrey Farrington £6.99
The Revenants – Geoffrey Farrington £3.95
The Book of Nights – Sylvie Germain £8.99
The Man in Flames – Serge Filippini £10.99
Days of Anger – Sylvie Germain £8.99
Infinite Possibilities – Sylvie Germain £8.99
The Medusa Child – Sylvie Germain £8.99
Night of Amber – Sylvie Germain £8.99
The Weeping Woman – Sylvie Germain £6.99
The Cat – Pat Gray £6.99
The Black Cauldron – William Heinesen £8.99
The Arabian Nightmare – Robert Irwin £6.99
Exquisite Corpse – Robert Irwin £14.99
The Limits of Vision – Robert Irwin £5.99
The Mysteries of Algiers – Robert Irwin £6.99
Prayer-Cushions of the Flesh – Robert Irwin £6.99
Satan Wants Me – Robert Irwin £14.99
The Great Bagarozy – Helmut Krausser £7.99
Confessions of a Flesh-Eater – David Madsen £7.99
Memoirs of a Gnostic Dwarf – David Madsen £8.99
Portrait of an Englishman in his Chateau – Mandiargues
£7.99
Enigma – Rezvani £8.99
The Architect of Ruins – Herbert Rosendorfer £8.99
Letters Back to Ancient China – Herbert Rosendorfer
£9.99
Stefanie – Herbert Rosendorfer £7.99
Zaire – Harry Smart £8.99

WEEK 1

1
FRIDAY

'All my friends were there, lying around in the garden. The cassette recorder was playing guitar music. My birthday's in August; at midnight I was twenty.'

The man raised his eyes from his knees, as if he expected some sign of agreement.

Cora Dulz gave him a throwaway nod and concentrated on the, as yet, unsullied white of her notebook.

'I was just like all the others. Nothing spectacular. Open-minded, no particular hang-ups, no particular ambitions. Childhood not specially hard, parents not specially rich. No hard drugs and not much in the way of neuroses, or talent either. Typical suburbs. Is smoking allowed?'

The psychiatrist put out an ash-tray. The man seemed nervous, almost at the end of his tether.

Arm. slk. sh. unir. gr. col. Cora noted, more to put on a show of activity than for any other reason.

'We were sitting under the fruit trees, talking about nothing in all possible variations. The temperature had dropped so that it was bearable. Not that it had been *so* hot you thought you'd get sunstroke. No!'

I'm being paid for this. Paid for it. Cora Dulz listened.

From a professional point of view the last few months had been terrible. Two patients had committed suicide, one after the other, as if by arrangement. At least neither of them had left their bills unpaid. A bit embarrassing in that kind of case to have to dun the bereaved. They always say, explicitly or implicitly, 'And you're demanding a fee *for that*?'

The man sitting there – pale, average height, held his cigarette with three fingers, like a pencil – was here for the first time. He had been squeezed in at the end of the day. The appointment had been liberated by one of the suicides.

Armani silk shirt; unironed; grimy collar. Cora checked out her abbreviations.

'Someone put on a cassette he had in the breast pocket of

11

his shirt. The conversation stopped for a moment, it was classical music, a soprano. A lot of the guests were unhappy with it. I waved them to shut up, told them it was my party, my birthday, it didn't matter what was played. The next moment something happened inside me, difficult to describe, a kind of shame at what I'd just said, that it didn't matter . . .'

The man leant forward. Not what you'd call handsome, interesting rather, with small eyes and a narrow face. You could tell by the marks on the bridge of his nose that he sometimes wore glasses.

'Some of the girls in the garden were very pretty . . . and yet . . . I just couldn't bear to listen to any of them any more. All the conversations had merged into a dull mumbling, incomprehensible, meaningless. I was listening to the soprano. It was as if her voice were drilling into my brain and illuminating every corner with a probe, a probe of light and sound. I felt light as a feather, I felt myself cut up into wafer-thin slices with cool air flowing between them. I know what you're thinking, but it *wasn't* drugs! A few beers, that's all . . .'

Gard. party. Birthd. Lots of beer.

'I've no idea what the voice was singing; could have been some Verdi. Suddenly I found all those sitting round me were getting on my nerves, so I stood up and took the recorder to the other end of the garden. No one followed me, otherwise I would have just kept on going.'

Remem. buy courg. & toms. for spag.

'It was marvellous in the dark. My friends were as far behind me as my childhood toys. I was filled with something new. As I said, it was my twentieth birthday. You imagine every round number must signify the beginning of a totally new epoch in your life. You're on the look-out for symptoms of change.'

'And this was how long ago?'

'Ten years and two weeks.'

Cora Dulz briefly wondered whether to offer her patient belated congratulations on this thirtieth birthday, but decided against it. Time was getting on, anyway.

'A live recording. From time to time there was applause,

much too loud, much too uproarious applause that, er . . . raped, yes, that's the word, *raped* the arias, the voice, that huge, magical, utterly indescribable voice, and then . . . Oh, sorry.'

Cigarette ash had fallen on the floor. The man bent down. Although his carelessness was getting on her nerves, the doctor brought out the usual phrases, don't bother, it doesn't matter. What she found even more unpleasant was the fact that the man was crawling round on the floor, perhaps glancing under the desk at her legs, which were covered in insect bites. When she got dressed that morning she had debated for a long time whether she should wear stockings despite the hot weather.

The man sat down again and stubbed out his cigarette, crushing the dog-end until the paper came away from the filter.

'Now where was I? Oh yes, I know, in the dark . . .' He hesitated. Presumably he would have liked to light another cigarette, but was put off by the little accident with the previous one. Cora took advantage of the pause to cast a quick glance at the registration form. Nagy was the man's name, Stanislaus Nagy. The box after 'profession' had been left empty. Very suspicious.

'I felt completely alone and I felt wonderful . . . The stars above loved me – you know the feeling? It's very rare. Then, suddenly . . .'

Nagy hesitated again, giving the doctor a sharp look, as if trying to decide how far he could trust her. His eyelids fluttered. He scratched the back of his neck.

Short of slp.? Pups. dilat. Ask paym. spot.

' . . . she was *there*. Emerged from the darkness and was standing before me, not ten paces away, in a white dress, whiter than you would think possible. She had her hair shoulder-length, and was wearing lipstick, just a touch. She simply stood there, looking upwards, not at the sky, more sideways, at the roof of the house, although I suspect our house just happened to be in her line of sight and she didn't actually see it at all. She didn't glance at me, not even for one second. Remarkable, don't you think? I mean, if you appear to someone, then you could at least glance at them, if only out of politeness. She didn't sing, didn't even move her lips, she simply stood there. It could be that I'd heard her name, perhaps even seen a picture of her somewhere, but the moment she appeared I knew exactly who she was. Her name descended from my brain to my tongue, and I whispered, *Maria!* If you think I stammered something like Maryandjoseph! and have just discarded the 'ndjoseph' over the years, you're wrong. Anyway, you can believe what you like, as far as I –'

'One moment, please. Let me get this clear. There was a voice coming from the cassette recorder, then a woman appeared to you. The woman whose voice was on the tape.'

'It was Maria Callas.'

'Callas.' Cora nodded non-committally and wrote down the name followed by:

White dr. Touch of mk.-up. Looking diag. upw.

From the windows of her consulting room on the seventh floor you could watch the people shopping or just strolling along St. Martin's Boulevard with its collection of outrageously expensive boutiques and cafes.

'Could you help me with some information. When was it Callas died?'

''77. Punk was just starting. Not that I think there's any connection.'

'Okay then. So she'd been dead for a few years. Was there anything in her appearance to suggest that? I mean, did she appear to you as a *young* woman?'

Nagy leant back in his chair and placed the tips of his fingers together. A suspicious frown flitted across his face.

'She looked, well . . . youthful. Difficult to be precise, perhaps twenty-five, perhaps thirty-five. Her face was radiant. I was . . . in shock. Incapable of standing up. Not really surprising, eh?'

'How long did the manifestation last?'

'Can't have been very long. There wasn't much left on the cassette and she vanished the moment the music stopped. Like a light going off. Press the switch and it's gone. I felt chilled to the bone, as if I'd fallen asleep in the garden and woken up in the morning, shivering with cold.'

'You discount the possibility that that is what actually happened?'

'Totally.'

'What next?'

'I started behaving as if I were nineteen again. The silence . . . it was too much for me. I stumbled back to where my friends were. *Did you see that?* I called out. What? Something – this was how I put it – *abnormal* . . .'

Nagy's lips twisted in disgust at the memory of his choice of word.

'Had anyone seen anything?'

'Stupid question! Of course not.'

'Why 'of course'?'

'Load of ignoramuses. Nothing but boom-boom music inside their thick skulls. They asked me why I'd gone all offended and buggered off to the bottom of the garden. And could they please have some *normal* music now? *Normal* music! Yeah, well, we spent the rest of the evening listening to *extremely normal* music. I told no one about it . . .'

'Let's stay with the manifestation.'

'Okay.'

'Did you feel sexually attracted to it?'

'My God . . .' Nagy assumed a bored expression. 'I know you have to ask these questions. I could work out every one in advance. It's just a pity we have to waste time on them.'

'So you feel this consultation is a waste of time?'

'Oh, don't get me wrong . . . I wouldn't want to offend you in any way . . . they're just preliminaries . . .'

'Leading where, in your opinion?'

'How should I know?' Nagy raised his hands then brought them together with a little clap in front of his face.

So why was he only coming to see her now, ten years after the incident?

At that he gave a charming smile, roguish even. Cora couldn't help responding to the friendly glance that accompanied it and noticed for the first time the unusual colouring of his eyes, a very dark blue, bordering on violet. She poked around in her notes with her pencil, then gave her patient a surreptitious glance. Nagy's smile had gone.

'Nothing happened for ten years. Ten years!' he repeated. The dead, he implied, had a very cavalier way with time.

'I hadn't done anything special with my life, but at least I did have a hobby. I went to record shops, collected Maria's recordings, bought big books about her, became an admirer . . . Not a fanatic, I must stress that. No, it was all very restrained. Nothing much to it at all. Until . . . until two weeks ago, that is . . .'

'On your birthday.'

'On my birthday. Yes . . .'

'A second manifestation?'

Nagy cleared his throat. He had noticed right away that she was starting to force the pace of the conversation. Almost simultaneously both looked at their watches. The forty-five minutes were up.

Cora's thoughts went to courgettes and tomatoes. Nagy stood up, thus ending the session of his own accord, which Cora found very obliging of him.

'Have you time to see me on Monday? In the afternoon? It has to be the afternoon because . . . I've been getting up late . . . during the last couple of weeks.'

2

Once a week, on a Friday, Cora cooked spaghetti for herself and her husband. To be more precise, she cooked once a week, always on a Friday and always spaghetti, with various vegetables and a reasonable assurance of success. If the weather was suitable, they ate out on the terrace. Robert would extract a candle from the jumbo pack and select a suitable wine.

'Tastes great.'

'Thanks.'

Cora's home: a terraced house within sight of one of the more exclusive residential areas. A springboard rather than a final resting place. Had it not been for the rents they had to pay for their prime-site offices, Robert and Cora Dulz would long since have been able to move to those green hills, not so far away, with their electric perimeter fence. As it was, despite double income and strict contraception, they were still waiting. Their situation was not helped by the fact that Robert, a tax consultant, had been forced to give up morning work because of a chronic weakness of the cardiac muscle, a convenient excuse in general. Among friends, and when Cora wasn't listening, he would enthuse about his physical inadequacies; they were something everyone should acquire, he would add.

Fred and Frith, their two castrated tomcats, were wallowing in the last of the sunshine by the leylandii hedge. They were both plump and gay and had loved each other since they were fluffy little kittens.

'Do you think I've got beautiful legs?'

'Let's see them.'

She didn't want him to see her legs covered in insect bites, so she poured him some more wine.

For months now the house had been infested with fruit-flies. However much she aired the place, flailed and swatted, sprayed poison, they still multiplied. There was something (what?) they found irresistible about the house. Every time Cora massacred a few with the fly-swatter, the rest would still be sitting there apathetically, as if to say, 'That's life . . .'

That spring Cora had had a pond dug in the garden and released a pair of cicadas (a free gift from the pet shop). They had been much appreciated by the tomcats.

'A man came for a consultation today. Maria Callas appeared to him in a vision.'

'Lucky man.'

Cora's sole passion was filling her house with tasteful furniture. But now there were no improvements to be made, every room had its ideal decor, had had for months. Whenever, almost in desperation, she looked for some small gap that could be filled, she found her thoughts kept being drawn to her husband.

Robert's face was so severe. Like a slab of slate, fissured and porous. One blow with a hammer and it would crumble.

'Do you want to have sex with me?'

'Sometimes.'

Cora thought about getting a parrot. With clipped wings but a hard beak. Who would win, the tomcats or the parrot?

The weekend. Longed-for and feared. Two Saturdays would be nice. Instead, the Saturday is followed by a Sunday which, since you've already done your resting, always turns out to be a bit too long. You have to force yourself to find some amusement to get you through the day.

'Aren't the tomcats ungrateful! Other cats come and rub against you. Ours only do it when they have ticks, if at all.'

'It's the way you feed them. They know they're going to get regular meals.' Robert had told her that often enough.

Cora was silent. Then she gave her finger and thumb a good lick and put out the candle.

Belgian fries friend

Brussels (Reuter): Furious at his attitude to the massacres in Ruanda, a Belgian killed his friend and then ate parts of the corpse. According to the police, 26-year-old Guillaume Portiez has confessed to strangling a 38-year-old man after an argument. He then fried parts of the corpse and ate them. The reason was to punish his friend for not taking the massacres in Ruanda seriously enough, he said.

3
MONDAY

'Even in the biggest of big cities there are moments of unexpected quiet. You're walking through the park at three or four in the morning and, although it's not raining nor particularly cold, there is not a single person to be seen. No junkies or courting couples, no tramps and no Peeping Toms at the gay meat-market. The place is like a ghost town, completely deserted. I like going for walks at night. That's what I did on my birthday, and I didn't feel lonely. On the contrary, it was so quiet, so wonderfully quiet, other people would have spoilt it. The pagodas and bridges in the park were tastefully illuminated, the grass was a plasticine grey and the half moon the colour of a slice of lemon. I sat down by the little river, staring at the sluggish blackness of the water and watching the wind blowing newspapers across the grass. Tattered scraps, the day's ragged army of overused words and phrases . . .

Do you have moments like that? You find yourself waking up in another world, and so close to yourself it makes you aware how far away from yourself you usually are? A kind of magic that gift-wraps your thoughts for you. Puts air-cushions under your feet. My thoughts were beautifully clear, not dashing round screaming at each other any more, but holding hands in an orderly crocodile . . . I felt marvellous. When I go for a walk in the park at night I carry a revolver in my pocket. I'm a bit of a romantic, but not stupid. That night it seemed paranoid. I had this rather dubious sense of security. I felt certain no one would come along, no one would disturb my birthday. The noise had died down and wouldn't start up again before first light.

Then suddenly, on the little mound beside the Temple of Apollo, a shimmer of light appeared. It grew into a strange glow from which a silhouette gradually emerged, then a figure, the figure of a woman in an off-the-shoulder silver dress, about a hundred yards away from me. A woman with long, dark hair. She stood there, motionless, and started to sing. She sang softly, very softly, but no doubt whose voice it was. And I knew *what* she was singing as well: roles that had made *her* famous. Norma. Tosca. Lucia. Only all of them – how can I explain it? – all of them *simultaneously*. Now there was a tune from one, now from another. If you listened carefully, it sounded as if there were many voices coming from her lips, but without giving the impression of a choir singing. No note sounded wrong, or out of place, it all blended into a celestial sound, familiar and yet at the same time like nothing you've ever heard before.

How many miles per day does the blood travel in your body? I don't know, but on a night like that it must do a couple of laps of honour extra. Maria was not directing her singing towards me – I could see her in half profile – nor did she accompany what she was singing with gestures, not even the slightest twitch, her arms just hung down limply at her sides. I haven't the slightest idea how long I spent crouching in the bushes.

Something deep inside me whispered I should get up and go to her, but I seemed to have been paralysed, my limbs felt like lead.

I was reminded of the innocent fool, Parsifal, who gapes at the goings-on and does not go to the aid of the Grail King. *Go to her aid. She needs your support.* Those were the kind of thoughts that filled my mind. I didn't ask, *Aid to do what? Support against whom?*

I summoned up all my courage and took three steps towards her. With every step I took the figure grew paler, lost more of its radiance and clarity. I threw myself to the ground, but it was too late. As if I had broken through some invisible barrier, the magic suddenly stopped, from one moment to the next there was nothing to be heard, nothing to be seen. The silence grabbed me by the collar and screamed, *Intruder!* The darkness planted itself in front of me like a young hooligan and said, *Come on then! Come on!* It was humiliating. It was illogical. I mean, if Maria's going to appear at all, then why should she accept me at a hundred yards, but not at eighty? What does she want? For me to listen to her?

Appreciate her voice? Okay. But her voice was very soft, I could have appreciated it much better from close to. Was I just a chance eavesdropper? Does Maria only notice unwelcome listeners within a certain radius? All speculation, and pretty grotesque at that, I know.'

Nagy was about six foot tall and of a slimness that would have done credit to a ballet dancer. His short, black, slightly curly hair, greying at the temples, had something of a renaissance painting about it, in particular of one of the Medicis, though Cora could not recall his name. She realised she had spent the Sunday looking forward to Nagy's visit. This obscure person had aroused an equally obscure affection in her. As he spoke, her resistance to him seemed to melt away and she was drifting along in a gondola. As if by magic her white coat had been transformed into an evening dress, the dress Nagy had described, off the shoulder, silver, the kind of dress that turned an ordinary woman into a fairy queen and a beautiful one into a goddess.

'Are you in love with Maria?'

'In love . . . that's one of those expressions. No . . . for me love is something like a distant star. It twinkles, it's definitely there, there's no denying that but, as Richard said to Cosima, it works out once every five thousand years — and that was only a hundred and thirty years ago, so how should I . . . ' He shrugged his shoulders.

Sometimes the patient did condescend to answer questions he clearly found tiresome but Cora suspected he was just saying what he assumed she wanted to hear so he could get back to talking about the things he found important.

'I was simply born too late, a programme error. I sometimes imagine travelling back through time, to the fifties, going up to her and saying, Maria! Come away with me and everything'll be okay. I know what you need, I'll be there for you. Forget Onassis. The money's not worth it.'

Cora could just sit back and listen. The patient reflected on his life of his own accord.

'I know. It's a strange fact that almost every man thinks

22

he could have made Maria Callas happy – or Marilyn Monroe or Dora Carrington, those women who got stuck with the wrong man. Almost every man thinks they'd had a raw deal from Life and he's the one who could have given them exactly what they needed to make up for it. But perhaps Life knew best. Perhaps these icons would never have given us so much beauty with some corny Mr Happy at their side.'

Cora, who was beginning to feel she ought to do something to justify her fee, went to the cupboard and brought over a folder with questionnaires, sheets with blobs of colour and rows of symbols. Nagy looked horrified.

'What are you going to do?'

'We could try catathymic association therapy. Starting with some yogic exercises to relax you.'

'This catathymic stuff – what's it for? I mean how does it work?'

'I give you a word and you tell me what comes into your mind.'

'What word?' Nagy's brow was furrowed.

'Any word. *Meadow*. Imagine a meadow. Describe it to me.'

The patient leant right back in his chair and closed his eyes.

'I see . . . it's summer, the meadow's been mown, it's brownish from the heavy oxides and there are amputated genitals lying around in the grass and . . . '

'Please be serious.'

'Two male ladybirds have tied a female ladybird up to a buttercup and . . . '

'And?' The psychiatrist made an effort to sound stern but was only partly successful.

'I'm sorry.' Nagy gesticulated wildly. 'It's no use. Not with me.'

'Okay, we won't then. What is it you actually want?'

'If I'm dumb enough to pay you money for this, then surely I have the right to ask *you* to give me the answer.'

'Do you want to get rid of the ghost?'

'For God's sake, no! What would there be left of me then?'

'But in that case –'

'Wait a moment, I'm not finished. Listen to me before you tear me out by the roots.'

At that moment Tamara, the receptionist, knocked twice and opened the door a crack to tell Cora that M. was sitting in the waiting room getting impatient. It was a long time since she had last overrun. Nagy gave her a rueful wink, sprang up from his chair and left without a word, but with a low bow.

4

Nagy: *Such an idealised vision is probably the physical manifestation of a longing for love from a female authority figure, i.e. his mother; it could be the expression of a demand for retrospective acceptance by his mother.*

I have the feeling I lost control of the situation slightly by letting the patient talk uninterruptedly for too long, thus allowing him to develop his delusion into a scenario he could impose on me. On the other hand, there is the danger he might break off the treatment should his desire to elaborate his delusion be frustrated. Despite his assertions to the contrary, he clearly lacks any sense of being ill. He needs someone to whom he can communicate, and thus legitimise, his abnormal perception.

Cora Dulz spoke her thoughts into the dictaphone and left it for Tamara to type out. Emerging from the lift into the golden street, she suddenly felt a strong urge to stroll around, the evening sun on her back, and spend money on things she didn't need. Her last patient of the afternoon had been Mulders, a type who was always on the verge of tears and thought he must be suffering from tantalism just because he had never thumped his father when his father had thumped him. Added to that were the failures of puberty, girls who had simply refused to respond to his overtures and whom Mulders now, decades later, wanted to kidnap and tie up, to achieve his belated end. He used to regale his psychiatrist with the details of his fantasies about these exploits – fortunately they would never be anything more than fantasies – until she began to feel like his defence counsel. After three sessions she had still been looking forward to the next. Not after fifty, though.

As she was sauntering from one shop-window to the next under the freshly whitewashed arcades, out of the corner of her eye she caught sight of someone waving from one of the tables outside the cafe at the opposite end of the esplanade. Since she had come quite a way from her office and Nagy, for that was who was waving, was sitting down at a table, she felt the suspicion he might have been lying in wait for her was probably unjust. Cora waved back, but turned round and set off in the opposite direction. She had to do that. She had to? She stopped, uncertain. It had taken just a few seconds for her principles to lose their point and their value. What she felt instead was delight, delight and a renewed belief in the rightness of coincidence. She turned round abruptly and, dispelling her last doubts with a brisk pace, went over to Nagy, who stood up and offered her a seat, a broad grin on his face. How irritating the way he refused to mouth the usual clichés about coincidence and it being a small world! He pushed the list of drinks across the table, just as if he had been expecting her, merely remarking that it would be a pleasure to enjoy the sunset in company. He had style.

The Café Claque was not far from the Opera and from it you could observe the queue of students outside the box office, waiting on the off-chance of getting unsold tickets at a reduced price. There were baguettes that were too big for a snack, cheap chardonnay and a waiter with Mexican good looks. Cora felt a slight queasiness in her stomach. Never before had she had anything to do with any of her patients outside her consulting-room. Nagy pointed to the Opera, saying he could repeat by heart the dates of every performance Callas had ever given there. Cora declined the offer, so Nagy kept his dates to himself and simply commented how good the wine was, only taking up the story of his visions when Cora asked him to.

'For a time I went to the park every night. Mostly in vain. People seemed to keep on finding new ways of making a racket. I got a bit worked up at times and set about the vagrants and druggies – even courting couples, but I'm sorry about that – with wild outbursts of swearing and cursing. Sometimes a kind of silence emerged. It may only have been for minutes, but that was enough. Maria would appear – in different costumes, by the way – but with each appearance her singing grew softer and softer until eventually it was scarcely comprehensible. As if all her strength were draining away. If anything with a vague resemblance to a human being should come along she would immediately disappear. A very fragile spell, I have to say. And the happiness, the rapture had left me. There was something eating away at me, lust and humiliation. I wanted to have Maria with me, help her, talk to her. I was no longer satisfied with the vision alone ... And then just recently, Monday morning in the pedestrian precinct ... by the fountain, the sky a delightful blue, everyone wearing pointed shoes and moving in slow motion. But under their faces – bones! Every mouth, even of the most beautiful woman, was twisted in a bony grin. And very strange sounds were coming from far above. Music, floating down like a butterfly that had died in flight. Then what did I see? Maria! Standing, like a preacher or a busker, in the middle of the throng, singing. And no one seemed to notice her apart from me. People brushed past her, some even went right through her. It didn't bother her in the least, but the moment I started to approach, hey presto! she was gone. It just wasn't true! In broad daylight!

Sometimes she appears in the middle of a crowd as a twelve- or thirteen-year-old girl. Don't get me wrong, I have no paedophile tendencies. I don't like it when she puts on her young girl act. It's as if she's disowning her career and everything she's achieved.'

Nagy's fingers were long and slim, and he buried them in the pockets of the overcoat he was wearing, a rather heavy one for the time of year. Leaning forward slightly in an attitude of caution and servility, his posture was that of a much older man. It conjured up thoughts of exile, loneliness, bitterness, unrequited love or at least brooding melancholy. Sometimes, however, his whole body would twitch and immediately his aura would change and he would exude youthful charm, verve, even arrogance or scarcely suppressed anger. A man, thought Cora, who was all too ready to put his cards on the table, yet seemed to keep changing his hand. Had she been asked to give a preliminary character sketch of her new patient based on his gestures, facial expressions and choice of phrase, the result would have been confusing, as if she had merged several people into one.

'What do you do for a living?'

'Detective. Not like in the cinema. A store detective.'

'Isn't that a horrible job?'

'How do you mean? Because you sometimes go shoplifting? No, seriously, you're right, it is horrible. Anyway, I'll soon have to start looking round for something else. Nowadays they have these electronic things hanging up everywhere that bleep if the tag hasn't been decoded. Soon they won't need store detectives any more. I can't say I'll be sorry. Every success you have, every *catch* has something degrading about it. And all the clichés are true.'

Depending on which expression he put on, Nagy seemed to be able to change his age at will, now he would be twenty, now forty, both equally convincingly. It also had something to do with his thin lips which, when he grinned or pouted, could become full and sensual. There was something similar about his eyes, which he often screwed up then opened wide in childlike wonder, showing off their curious coloration. One moment he was a young man from a good family, the next a failure surrounding himself with relics from better days. His coat, for example: very stylishly cut, definitely not off the peg, but with worn or grubby patches. And his shoes would by now certainly have forgotten all about Italy.

'Of course you get offers to forget the matter in return for sex. You wouldn't believe what women who have been caught red-handed are capable of, men too . . . and sometimes you behave irrationally; that is, the woman who's been caught shoplifting has irresistible arguments, makes you an offer you can't refuse, as they say in gangster films . . .'

Nagy's four-to-five-days' growth gave him a rather brutal, disreputable look. By contrast, the almost immaculate light-blue Armani suit looked like the disguise of a Russian anarchist from the pre-revolution days.

'Some women stuff things up their . . . you know what. And some undress and take the stuff out before my very eyes, even though there is a female colleague I could call. Disgusting.'

28

The sun disappeared behind the pediment of the Opera.

A gaudy, crucified Christ, painted in the style of Roy Lichtenstein, stared out from an advertising hoarding.

Nagy asked Cora whether she had ever been in a department store at night. Did she fancy trying it? The store was only a few streets away. It was worth seeing, all that space, a deserted temple to consumption by emergency lighting, the huge windows on the top floor . . .

Cora was attracted by Nagy's offer. It awakened childhood dreams in her. Would Robert be worried? Why should she care?

She could ring him up. She thought about it, but didn't bother. Let him suffer, just a little.

'There's no problem? We can go just like that?'

'You'd really like to?'

Nagy's eyes were round and shining. No problem at all, he said, he was well in with the security guards, some of them even brought their whole families along, grandma and all. Some nights it was like Disneyland in there.

He walked half a pace in front of her, his hands clasped behind his back and a spring in his step. Cora was not too happy with the situation. She was already beginning to regret having agreed to go, but couldn't think of a way of calling the visit off without appearing irresolute and thus losing authority. Without warning, Nagy suddenly stopped. They could take their time, he told her, the cleaning women would still be in the store. He went over to an ice-cream stall gaudy with neon lights – it was almost dark – and asked her what her favourite flavours were. Cora hesitated. She was close to diving into a taxi to escape, and bugger her authority.

'Malaga.'

'And?'

'Cherry.'

'I knew it!'

Nagy handed her the cone with a nonchalant smile that made resistance impossible.

'I know what you're thinking. You're thinking it's not right for a psychiatrist to be wandering round the town at night with her patients, far away from her couch and notebook. Don't try to deny it.'

'No, you're right.' Cora remembered therapeutic guidelines which advised keeping one's distance in this kind of situation. 'To be honest, I don't know if I really want this ice-cream.'

That made her feel better, then, when a look of heartrending sadness crossed Nagy's face, cruel. His expression so affected her that she felt she was floating on the edge of sleep, the way you sometimes do in the morning, when you know you're awake, but still roll over onto the other side to slip back into the previous night's dream.

'Don't you like it? You could at least try it.'

'Okay, okay. It tastes great. Let's get on.'

The crossroads were blocked by a paraglider who had crashed. To be precise, it wasn't the glider who was blocking the road, but all the vans with blue lights flashing that had arrived too late to save him. Recently the number of lunatics throwing themselves off skyscrapers had reached epidemic proportions. A few years ago they would have gone to see an analyst. Now they jumped. The question was, how did they manage to get onto the roofs unnoticed, lugging their paragliders?

For a while neither of them said anything. They strolled round the outside of the huge Pullam's Department Store, the showpiece of an architect who had originally specialised in ecclesiastical buildings. Nagy pointed out the illuminated porter's lodge in the rear entrance. Sitting there was a fat, middle-aged man in a blue uniform. The cleaning women, almost all of them from Asian countries, were clustered round the delivery entrance, ready to leave. A foreman was shuffling lists. The fat security guard gave Nagy a wave.

'A guided tour is it then?'

'Yes. Have you the schedule of patrols?'

'Of course. Not many on duty tonight. Heading for the BFD?'

'Not this time. Thanks.'

Nagy, holding a piece of paper like a handkerchief, ushered

her into the building with an elaborate bow. Cora gave the uniform a brief nod and entered. Nagy closed the glass door behind her.

'What's the BFD?'

'A stupid joke.'

'Well explain it.'

'Oh . . .' Nagy sighed, clicking his tongue to show how embarrassing he found the whole thing.

'The bed department.'

'Oh. I see.'

'No . . . It's just the kind of thing people say. I mean, our bedroom furniture department's very luxurious, some of the suites cost six month's salary, so sometimes one of the security guards'll treat himself to forty winks on one. Or someone's had a bit of a tiff at home and prefers to doss down here, these things happen.'

'Have you taken women to the BFD?'

'Do you ask out of personal or professional interest?'

Cora couldn't repress a grin and Nagy, having got out of having to answer, pressed the lift button for the ninth – the top – floor.

'Sports equipment, electrical goods, restaurant', he said in the mechanical tone of lift-boys from ancient films.

The special thing about the top floor was the huge windows with their sides sloping at different angles that allowed you to see out over half the city. To the left was the end of the central park, in the middle the old town, beyond it the docks and the sea, to the right the business district, the opera house, the pedestrian precinct and, only faintly visible, industrial areas, as far as the prefab suburbs way out to the north. Some of the buildings had pretty floodlighting, which made particular sense in the winter when the homeless could keep warm beside the powerful lights. There were lamps hanging from trees, making a network of bright spots across the park. If you had good eyesight, and a vivid imagination, you could see large ocean-going steamers in the hazy distance. Red lights flashed a warning from the top of the television tower. Most of the skyscrapers were hidden from view since the panoramic windows were only on the side facing the sea. Cora wondered whether the skyscrapers also had to have warning lights, she'd never thought of looking to see. She asked Nagy whether he knew. He didn't. He was also too busy trying out a golf club. He appeared to have a practised swing: strong, elegant and just a bit affected.

'Do you play regularly?'

No, Nagy replied, he was completely unathletic. He never played any games himself, though he did watch quite a few people he had dealings with. Did she fancy a cigarette?

They sat down, staring at the city spread out below them, let the ash fall onto the floor and stubbed out their cigarettes on the arms of the bench. Nagy got up and went off, without a word, leaving Cora unsure what was happening. He was gone for almost ten minutes while Cora just sat there feeling stupid. What if one of those 'patrols' should turn up? He had a nerve! Finally he came back with two quarter-bottles of Moët & Chandon and glasses to match. He refused to say where he had got them. Cora decided it would be only polite to accept the offer.

'But what if I couldn't stand champagne? You'd have put me in an awkward situation.'

Nagy bowed his head in acquiescence, at the same time grinning like a charmer who knows he can get away with almost anything.

The emergency lighting was not dissimilar to a full moon on a cloudless night and gave the yawning gangways between the shelves a suggestion of forbidden zones. Ghostly. Dream architecture.

As a teenager Cora had often gone shoplifting in department stores. Lipsticks, fashion magazines, lingerie. She had never been caught, but had still given it up eventually. She imagined being caught by a store detective like Nagy and, ready to do anything to avoid a scandal, . . . her thoughts ran riot. It was fun. Nagy was pointing at something.

'Down there, in the park. That's the Temple to Apollo. Next to the mound.'

Cora looked where he was pointing. Yes, there was a

temple. No doubt about it. But why should Nagy sound as if that was proof of Maria Callas's posthumous appearances?

'I can hear her singing! A long way off. Can you hear it too?'

A faint light appearing at the far end of the vast floor silenced them. They could hear the chink of glasses, scraps of conversation.

Nagy suggested they should go back down. Over there – he pointed to the light – the bosses were having a party. The way he said it made it sound very mysterious, very dangerous.

'If you've got children, we can go past the wine gum counter on the way back and take a bag of them. On the house.'

'I haven't got any children.' Cora found Nagy's method of getting personal information out of her rather sneaky, but did she *have* to answer him? She thought about it. It was certainly crazy to accept the trip to the store. But it was exciting, too. The danger would come when Nagy paid her his first compliment. Despite his gallant manner, he had held back on that so far. Cora was a bit disappointed. Did she think of herself as attractive? On her last birthday, her thirty-seventh on the trot, she had looked at herself in the mirror for a long time until she was happy with what she saw. She wasn't what you'd call a beauty, but there was something about her which attracted men – especially men who had at one time wanted to sleep with one of their teachers.

After she had qualified Cora had decided she needed a serious image to go with her consulting rooms, had exchanged her contact lenses for glasses, stopped dying her hair and painting her nails or wearing lipstick. Her sex life was restricted to those rare moments when hormonal hyperactivity in her husband happened to coincide with her own biological urges.

They were in the electrical goods department, sitting on the sofa where customers could listen to CDs. In spite of the sinister lighting there were shadows on the move everywhere. Or perhaps not. Silence, honeycombed with imagined sounds, enveloped them, cried out for noise, talk to drown it out, breathing to blow it away.

Two glasses of chardonnay and now the champagne, Cora's bloodstream was accustomed to a low alcohol intake . . . and then there was the high ceiling, the endless space . . . a torrent of confused feelings cascaded through her, to be registered or soaked up subcutaneously, moments that washed up enough flotsam and jetsam to build a ship.

'How do you feel?'

'Couldn't rightly say.'

'Shall I show you a trick?'

'Hmmmm?'

Nagy clicked his fingers and, like a magician producing the correct playing card, was holding a small photo in his hand.

'Maria drinking an espresso in a café. My favourite picture of us.'

'A neat trick. Why do you say 'of us'?'

Nagy frowned, about to say something, then clicked his fingers again and the photo vanished.

'Yes . . . yes, that's true, I've not quite perfected the trick yet.'

He's my patient. My *patient*, she had to remind herself. So far nothing remarkable had happened. She felt like telling him about her shoplifting past but didn't. It was too long ago. As if by magic two more quarter-bottles appeared from his coat pockets.

If ghosts really existed, he said, the stores would be full of them. People who had been snatched away before they had managed to spend all their money and now haunted the cash-desks at night, full of unsatisfied consumer longings.

'But why did you say, *if ghosts really existed*? You know one personally.'

Nagy gave her a baffled look. 'Oh, yes!' And he laughed. Laughed out loud for no obvious reason, so loud that Cora got up and went over to the lift. She couldn't stand it there any longer. The alcohol had merely anaesthetised her apprehensiveness, not got rid of it. In one second her mood had changed completely. All this was impossible.

Unprotesting, Nagy set off after her, slipping into the lift like Cora's shadow. Only when they were out in the open air again did he suggest they carry on walking for a while. To the south was the old town, or, to be more precise, the three streets lined with antique shops and junk dealers. It was still warm. The cluttered windows meant there was no question of boredom, even if the flow of conversation had shrunk to a dribble.

Cora and Nagy turned into a dimly lit side-street. Lying on the grille over the steps down to a cellar was a naked man, young and not unattractive.

'Do you fancy him?' asked Nagy as they walked past, then, when Cora shrugged her shoulders, 'Would you like to have him?'

Cora denied it. And said no to all the other young men at the roadside.

'Look! There! The top shelf!'

From the age of four until she was seven Cora had had a musical box on her bedside table. On the lid, in pointed shoes, white tutu, leotard and tights, was a little ballerina which moved in time to the tune. Her hands clasped above the silver crown on her head, the princess on the musical box had twirled her way into Cora's heart. The little girl who refused to go to sleep without her musical-box melody, without the tinkling notes, each of which was one step further into the realm of Morpheus, which in Cora's imagination was somewhere that was always just above her head; a realm you did not plunge into, but wound your way up to.

When, one evening, the musical box stopped, its works fell apart and her father's screwdriver rendered the damage irreparable, a new musical box was bought, with a similar ballerina and the tune of 'Somewhere over the rainbow'. The magic was gone, spoilt for good.

For a long time after the loss of the musical box Cora had suffered from insomnia. Even now, thirty years later, no image from her childhood was as clear in her memory as that of the pirouetting princess.

It was the same model. She was sure. God, how grateful she felt towards Nagy just for this chance find!

'The musical box?'

'Yes. I had one. I've been looking and looking, but . . .'

Nagy asked if she would like to have the musical box. Definitely, she replied, she'd have to come first thing tomorrow morning, when the shop opened, so no one else could snap it up.

Her slim, almost frail-looking patient knocked on a dustbin behind him. It made a dull sound; the aluminium was well-filled.

'If I have come to realise one thing, it's that you can go quite a bit farther than people would have you believe.'

It was all over so quickly. Nagy picked up the dustbin with both hands and ran, holding the bin out in front of him, straight through the window. There was a tinkle of glass and an alarm started up. Nagy laughed, brandished the musical box triumphantly and jumped back down into the street. 'I suggest we go for a little jog, hmm?'

Cora Dulz had not run for years. Without a syllable of protest, struck dumb by a combination of bewilderment and horror, she set off at a fair pace. She felt frightened, but the feeling was more like the pleasant tingle of watching a tightrope walker on the wire than actual fear. Only gradually did true realisation of what had happened dawn on her and even then she shut her eyes to it, without even a flicker of self-reproach. She would have laughed if there had been enough breath left in her lungs for laughing. The two of them dashed hither and thither through the maze of streets and alleyways in the old town. Nagy kept on hanging back, urging Cora on, the musical box clamped under his arm like a rugby ball. Finally they shot into the darkness of a multi-storey car-park and tore up several ramps before dropping to the ground between two all-terrain vehicles, panting and gasping for breath. A touch on the button and their wheezing was accompanied by the musical box, something from *Le Postillon de Longjumeau*, long-forgotten music, metallic, jangling and slightly out-of-tune, which only made it even more magical. Cora leant over to Nagy and gave him a kiss; he raised his eyebrows and smiled. She wriggled up close to him and, still gasping for breath, lay with her head resting on his thigh in expectation of caressing hands, an embrace; she was ready for him, longing to feel the touch of his fingers. He, however, remained motionless, staring up at the ceiling, the palms of his hands flat on the floor.

A smell of metal and petrol.

'What have you done?' Cora asked. Implied in the tense she chose for her question was another: 'And why are you doing nothing now?'

The sharp silhouette of his head came closer until it was inches from hers. Cora parted her lips, pushing the lower one out a little so he could see how it was trembling, sending out signals of desire and expectation. She half closed her eyes and squinted, breathing audibly, at the head, which had paused, its hesitation sending a quiver through her whole body. Then the silhouette leant back, swaying pensively from side to side, an unfathomable outline. Cora wanted to say – wanted to scream out, *What's the matter? Why don't you kiss me? Do you want to see me wriggling on the hook? Do you want me to beg for it?*

'You're not a happy woman.'

It appeared to be the least erotic thing the silhouette could think of to say. Cora stood up and fiddled with her hair. 'What business of yours is that?'

'None at all, no, I'm sorry. It's just that you'd like to have sex with me now and –'

'Who says so?'

'– it's not on because . . . Don't take offence! There are some people you want to pour your heart out to, but you don't go any farther, and that's right. Did I excite you that much?'

'You conceited – !'

'Now, now. Remember, I'm just your patient . . . round the bend . . .' Stanislaus Nagy grinned as he tapped his forehead.

'I've got to go home.'

'Yes. That would be the sensible thing to do.'

'You're late get'n home . . .'

Extraordinary how many identifiable sounds Robert managed to accommodate between his grunts and yawns.

'Should have phoned. Sorry.'

'Since when've you start'd sayinsorry?' Suspicious rumblings. 'You havin naffair?'

'Whatever for? When I've got you.' She climbed into bed and arranged her pillow, listening to Robert's sighs and groans as he tried to get into the most comfortable position for sleeping. Half past one, said the phosphorous on the clock face. Moonlight was falling onto the bedcover, there was a bluish pool below the window.

'Do you love me?' Cora whispered the question into the dark, where it hung around, uncertain what to do.

'Luvyoutoo . . .'

Dead Diver Found on Mountain Top

Munich: Following forest fires on the Greek island of Thassos the body of Munich scuba-diver Noah L. was found among burnt-out tree-trunks on the top of a mountain. The mystery was, he was wearing full diving equipment! It took months of investigation to establish what happened. Noah had been diving off the coast of Thassos, just at the time when fire-fighting aeroplanes were filling up with water, and he got sucked up into the water chambers. The pilots did not notice, and emptied their tanks over the forest fire in the mountains.

'Look at all these people. They make no demands on life that can't be satisfied with a full belly, a nice house and three orgasms per week. Plus health, death taking its time and good programmes on the box. And who can blame them? But when you remember that all the world's a stage, it's simply a non-starter. The human contract states we have to be actors for all and audience for all. And boredom's never very far away . . .'

The good ones kill themselves, the rest end up on my list! Cora Dulz had not forgotten Nagy's rejection of her a couple of days ago and was determined to keep staring straight past him, stony lipped, as he leant against the window-ledge of her consulting room, loftily holding forth in philosophical vein. She didn't quite manage it. Nagy seemed to have changed in some way. As if it were bathed in a different light, his face had the effect of a work of art that you think has been created for you alone and must contain some message concerning your future life.

'As a girl Maria was fat, bloated, unprepossessing. I'm well aware of that, you mustn't think I want to idealise her. On the contrary, that's precisely what I find intriguing about her, the trauma of the ugly duckling that is still faintly visible underneath the swan. The humanity which resists any attempt to see her as a saint. If that weren't the case, I wouldn't find her interesting at all.

Booed off the stage and spat upon, called a witch, a female Cagliostro trying to sell shit for gold by a group of critics who sat in judgment on her – all that is part of her, and a necessary part, just as an icon has to go through a urine bath. I followed her everywhere, even when she sang in a church, I'm not such a stickler as you might think.'

This last sentence Cora found disconcerting, but she ignored it. Enough of listening, it was time for something else, she decided.

'What was your relationship with your mother like?'

'I didn't come here to talk about that kind of rubbish.'

'You didn't?'

'I was brought up by my grandmother.'

'Aha!' Cora was already mapping out the lines of a future therapy.

'No! Nonsense! It was a joke.'

'What then?'

'I have a confession to make.'

'Yes?'

Nagy sat down and in posture and gesture was transformed into a primary-school teacher.

'I lied to you. In almost everything I said. With the best of intentions. I wanted to . . . to prepare you for me, so to speak . . .'

Cora raised her eyebrows, more out of politeness than anything else, then thought better of it and lowered them again so as not to put the patient under pressure with an exaggerated show of expectation.

'First of all, I'm not thirty.'

'But?'

'Older.'

'How much older?'

'Much, much older.'

'Could you put a figure to it?'

'No. I don't know. Really I don't.'

'But –'

'I'm not a store detective either, I may be down-at-heel, but I'm not that desperate. At least it's not my main occupation. I've never lived in a house and certainly not one with a garden. And never had any friends. Never.'

This time Cora's brows went up spontaneously.

'Every person has some friends.'

'Exactly.'

There was a silence. Cora had no idea what Nagy was trying to tell her.

'And the apparition?'

'Hmm . . . How shall I put it? Maria . . . I do see her, only . . . it's whenever I want to. And I want to often. Then she's

40

standing there, far away, untouchable, almost the way she was when she still had a body. She's not dead and she's not alive. She's somewhere up there, with the icons, in a place the other side of longing. I knew Maria well, although she was totally unaware of it.'

Nagy stared at the cheap print of Van Gogh's *Sunflowers*, apparently gathering his strength for what was to come next. There was a forced smile on his face, frozen, almost corpse-like, then a quiver went through his shoulders, ran over his chin to the corners of his mouth and came to a halt in a frown on his forehead.

'My name is not Stanislaus Nagy, or, rather, that's only one of the many pseudonyms I go under.'

He made an overdramatic pause, then fixed his gaze on the psychiatrist. 'It was love at first sight.'

'What? With me?'

'No. *Her.* Maria.'

'But . . .'

'Wherever she was, I was there too, one way or another. The fact that she was human, that she died and slipped away from me, is tearing me apart; it's my trauma, it's almost killed me. I'm still alive, but only just. What you see before you is merely a shrivelled shell. I don't expect help from you, nor comfort. I just need someone I can tell everything, someone who will have to listen to me because that's their job.'

Flattered, curious, understanding or expectant, Cora Dulz could not decide which of her faces to put on. The result was a postmodern mishmash.

'It was fairly early on in her life that I became interested in Maria. Long before she ever appeared on the stage. I don't know why. It was a premonition . . .'

'What is it you wanted from her?'

'I collected good singers.'

'Of course . . .' Cora tried another approach. 'How old were you *at the time*?'

'No older than I am now.'

'That's no answer.'

'Oh yes it is. And a profound one at that.'

'I don't think so. Would you like to talk about your childhood?'

'I never was a child. In the beginning I was a thought. Later on came images. The images became flesh. At some point or other the process of personification was . . . was overdone, probably. Nowadays there is hardly anything to distinguish me from the idiot you think I am.'

'But I don't think you're an idiot.'

'You think I'm sick, and you're right to do so. I am sick. But perhaps I'm one of those people who are destroyed if they're healed.'

'I think it's time you told me who you are.'

Nagy stood up, clasped his hands behind his back and bowed his head. 'Well . . . I'm the Devil . . . at least, that's what people call me . . .'

Cora went along with it. 'Why didn't you say that right away?'

'You'd have thought I was mad.'

'But that's my job!'

She was still hoping her patient had made it all up, was having a rather extended joke at her expense. She found it difficult to accept that he was every bit as deranged as he appeared to be.

'I don't enjoy evil any more. Everything's so boring. Every day you can hear in the news about torturers who are much more imaginative than me. May I make an embarrassing confession?'

'What?'

'It's unworthy of the Devil, sentimental, mawkish. It'll almost make you feel sorry for me. You won't take me seriously any longer if I tell you . . .'

'Get on with it!'

'I'd like to be affectionate towards someone, just for once. Touch them with my fingertips, whisper to them softly, sweet nothings, every syllable a kiss brushing against their cheek. I'd like to caress someone, bewitch them, spoil them, fool around with them, a romantic song on my lips – I find the whole idea incredibly tempting. I've committed so many cruelties, filled the history books with so many atrocities, thought up such diabolical scenarios, just for once I'd like to be different, a lover, a poetry-writing, cloak-over-the-puddle-spreading, vow-stuttering, kitsch-peddling, love-blind something. It's enough to make even the Devil blush, don't you think?'

Cora concentrated on her notebook. 'It all depends . . .'

'If you feel your heart-strings fluttering, you're no use as a devil any more. Sometimes I think Maria wanted me to slough my skin, as if something different might appear, instead of more snakes.'

He lit a cigarette and inhaled so avidly craters appeared in his cheeks.

'I appeared before her as an admirer asking for an auto-graph. Which she gave me, but nothing more, no real smile, no shake of the hand. I approached her in various guises – waiter, lift-boy, journalist, jet-setter – but none was any help. She always had the feeling there was something not quite right about me. We only had to be together for a few seconds and her brow would wrinkle slightly, her eyes narrow and she would dispose of me like the most tiresome of routine engagements. Maria could be cruel. She once told me – I was a young aristocrat in a white blazer – I exuded a pungent odour which gave her a headache, then simply turned on her heel and left me standing there. As if I'd been bathing in blood and sulphur! It might be very healthy, but it's not something I'm in the habit of doing. I've a reputation to keep up! Even now it still drives me mad. Am I mad?'

He leant forward over the table.

'As mad as anyone in my profession could wish.'

'There you are. I'm not paying you for nothing. What do you intend to do?'

Cora made an indeterminate gesture, something between 'how should I know' and 'we'll have to see'. Nagy's eyes were boring into her cheeks, which were burning.

'To a whole generation she meant intoxication, a *frisson*, an icy glissando down the spine; her voice was the essence of love distilled into an acoustic phenomenon – I assume *you* don't listen to Callas records?'

'No, I . . .'

'That was important for me. I wanted to tell my story to someone who wouldn't be giving me understanding nods all the time. You've probably never got really worked up about anything in your whole life . . . Am I right?'

'Let's stick to the subject,' was Cora's reply, which came closer to answering yes than she really wanted. She was quite keen on furniture, as was pointed out earlier. As a teenager she'd had a bit of a crush on Robert Redford; and imitated Debbie Harry.

'If one's yearning is so strong, even though its object is unattainable – isn't that irrational? Isn't that madness? Or perhaps it isn't? Perhaps it's extremely rational behaviour, because you're using it to conceal some other failure? The world doesn't need me any longer. I should have left when God went. He always was a better loser. How about a meal? There's this new Abkhazian restaurant with lovely little tables.'

Cora, as if she had no will of her own, meekly nodded.

Dead woman travelled on bus for hours – no one noticed

Venice (epd): All afternoon a dead woman drove back and forward in the bus in the harbour town of Mestre by Venice, and no one noticed! It was not until just before midnight – the vehicle had been standing in the depot for some time – that a cleaner discovered the dead body. 72-year-old Maria Zuliani Vitturi took the bus to go and visit her sister, but had a stroke on the way there and died. During the course of the afternoon several unsuspecting passengers, obviously deceived by the 'sleeping' woman's peaceful expression, sat next to her. The driver did not notice her at all. After the end of his shift he locked the bus and went home, leaving the dead body sitting there.

'Maria grew up in New York, then returned home to Athens with her mother and sister – her father was a fly-by-night and glad to see the back of his family. Strategically the move was not a very felicitous decision. The country was invaded by Italian forces, and when they made a mess of it the Germans stepped in. On 27 April, 1941, Athens was occupied. That was about the time Maria first came to my attention, when she caught my eye, or, to be more precise, my ear. In visual terms she was a rather unsightly phenomenon, shapeless and spotty, a land fill site for chocolates, bursting at the seams and with no marriage prospects. If anyone had told me I would become enslaved to this incarnation of the force of gravity to the point of madness, I would have laughed them off stage.'

The waiter lit the candles and served a selection of typical Abkhazian hors d'oeuvres. Among the small print on the label of the wine bottle was a Soviet star.

'Still, there was something attractive about her. The first person to admire her not yet fully developed voice was an Italian ensign, who gave her a portion of his rations. Having sung for her supper, she hid under the stairs and ate the lot, without saving anything for her mother and sister. I liked that. Maria was a daydreamer, hungry and ugly. And brave. In the early summer of '41 the German occupation forces banned any kind of noise-making, public or private. On the evening of the day the decree was announced, Maria pushed the piano out onto the balcony of their penthouse flat in Patissiou St. and played and sang for all she was worth, to the loud applause of the passers-by, Greeks, Italians, even Germans. Maria was sixteen and just starting to develop her repertoire, driven on by her ambitious mother, who reserved all her love for her other, prettier daughter, but had decided early on that Maria must become famous, world famous, in order to support the family over the coming decades. Talent was there, no doubt about that, but how great was only evident to what you might call the *visionary* ear. Her talent was helped by the evening curfew, which got her into the habit of staying at home and working on her voice. I did my part by ensuring that the curfew was not lifted during the whole of the period of occupation. I also decided to get rid of her awful mother.'

'Why?'

'Why not? An opportunity turned up quite soon. One night a Greek Air Force officer, a friend of the family, brought two Britons who were on the run. Evangelia, Maria's mother, was uncertain whether to take them in or not. The occupying Germans had imposed martial law and it was a capital offence. However, being infected with a quasi-religious patriotism, she did. The woman had fallen into my trap. The two Britons moved into the smallest of the five rooms, and when they listened to the BBC at night, Maria would play loud music on the piano so that nothing could be heard outside. After a while I wrote a letter to the German commandant and then let things take their course. That was my mistake.'

Nagy picked at his food apathetically and left most of it. Cora wondered why the slices of steamed kohlrabi tasted of pear. She had chosen a grill for her main course and it had come surrounded by an enormous quantity of parsley. Kurdish influence?

'Someone tipped the Britons off. The friend of the family collected them and carted them off somewhere. The next morning an Italian patrol came crashing in through the door. The escapees had left letters and photographs lying around, still enough for the death sentence. And what happens? Maria sits down at the piano and sings arias from *Tosca*. The Italians lower their rifles, sit down in a semicircle round the piano and listen with rapt attention. Forget they're supposed to be searching the flat! Unbelievable? I thought so too when I heard it. I sensed there was something going on. I wasn't the only one who had noticed Maria. She wasn't just my toy any more. He was joining in.'

'Who do you mean by 'he'?'

'Well . . . *Him*. You know.'

'God?'

Nagy gave an exasperated nod and a sideways look up at the ceiling. Cora put on her enthusiastic act.

'You know God personally?'

'We tend to avoid each other.'

'What does he look like?'

Nagy made a gesture to say he found the subject disagreeable.

'We haven't seen each other for a while now. The last time he looked pretty old. He'd had enough of the world. May I proceed?'

'Please do.'

She felt as if her patient meant some things seriously and others not, as if he were playing with her emotions and instincts, exposing or concealing himself as the mood took him. There was no system behind it that she could see, and it went beyond the natural vanity of a sick person requiring respect as well as protection and help. Nagy wanted more than respect, he demanded constant amazement. And if the psychiatrist was not prepared to give it, if a sarcastic remark slipped out, or even if she asked too 'profane' a question, he would immediately get uptight and look away in pique.

'The next day the Italians returned, and the following days. This time they knocked, and they brought bread, salami and macaroni for the family. I have always believed in the power of song (who has all the good tunes?) but that was going too far. It was beginning to have that gooey, christmassy feel I can't stand. I came close to withdrawing from Maria's life and leaving the field to *him*.' Again he shot a sideways glance up at the ceiling. 'At the time Maria did not seem to me to be of vital importance. But then . . . it's difficult to explain . . .'

Get on with it! You've worked out the story in advance.

'Something drew me back to Athens, to Patissiou St. It was July. At night Maria practised *Tosca* on the balcony and I, sitting on a roof a few houses away, responded by taking the part of Cavaradossi. It was beautiful . . .'

'Do you play an instrument?'

'Rarely.'

'Which?'

47

'Any. Why?'

'Just asking.'

'Hm . . .' Slightly irritated, Nagy took a sip of his wine.

'The people of the district listened spellbound to our long-range duets and tried to find out who the Cavaradossi was. A fantastic July! Especially since hearing her young, exciting voice like that spared me the sight of her bloated sound box of a body. You have to imagine it: Maria's voice was like the first crocus peeping through the snow, the first ray of sunshine piercing your eyelids after a nightmare, the unearthly glow of a refracted colour. Whenever the world war allowed, I went to Athens to savour the way she was developing. And played a few tricks to combat any danger of pompousness. That's just my nature, I couldn't help it. All harmless stuff, really. Anything more serious *he* would probably have sabotaged anyway. The rules of the game were already set, dammit! My scope for action was restricted. To give you an example, I made the soprano who was to sing Tosca at the Athens opera ill. Maria was asked if she would step in. Of course she would! The original soprano – I did rather keep on at her – went half crazy. She hated Maria. Too ill herself to do anything about it, she sent her husband. He was to spoil Maria's entrance simply by blocking her way onto the stage at the appropriate moment. Cheap farce, you'll say.' Nagy grinned from ear to ear. 'I enjoyed it. So as not to miss her entrance, Maria flung herself at the man and scratched him all over the face. He, no gentleman himself, thumped her with his fist. To cut a long story short, she made her entrance, but with a black eye which, fortunately, was obscured by her hat. I liked her. The audience did too. They were literally swept away by the passion of the seventeen-year-old Tosca. The applause was rapturous. A new star had appeared in the firmament. Not a supernova yet, but still –' He beamed and smacked his lips with relish.

'In October '44 the Germans left Athens. By then I was bored to death with the war. Everything had become so technical, there was no room for flair any longer. The things that went on – and I had no hand in them – were crude and vulgar.

For the first time I had the feeling the human race didn't really need me any more, they could manage quite well on their own. They took over my role in the great game, only were more cruel and more single-minded than it would ever have occurred to me to be. It was the start of what you would call a 'crisis of meaning'. To take your mind off it you indulge in whims, in little obsessions which grow into big obsessions. That's what happened to me with Maria. I suddenly found that without realising it I had become hooked on something, the way an unemployed man gets hooked on alcohol. Never before had I allowed my desire for beauty so much free rein. But then destruction was breaking all known records. There had to be a balance, a countercurrent . . .'

Nagy's main course, a kind of spinach soufflé with veal rissoles, lay untouched on the table in front of him. As if to keep up appearances, he swallowed three mouthfuls and pushed his plate aside, more relieved to get it out of the way than because he was full.

'Where was I? Oh yes. Athens celebrated the liberation and civil war promptly broke out. The communist resistance refused to disband, to give up its weapons, and started a rebellion against the new government. There was a blood-bath in the capital. Devil take it! I was concerned for Maria's safety. It was just a crummy little war that thought it could make the big time. Thousands were killed, Maria's uncle among them. And Patissiou St. was in no man's land between the fronts. Maria couldn't practice when there was the thunder of mortar fire outside and volleys of machine-gun fire thudding into the wall of the house. One night the cage with their canaries was hit. All that was left of the birds were a few scraps of flesh and feathers. And there was fighting on the roofs as well. I did everything I could to bring it to an end as quickly as possible, but my influence over that kind of thing is more limited than you might think. Day and night explosions, sirens, screams. Finally I lost patience, disguised myself as a British messenger and led the three women right through the middle of the shooting to the safety of the embassy buildings. Just imagine it! Me, the noble boy scout! It was, moreover, the first and last

49

time Maria accepted help from me. She didn't recognise me, well, perhaps she had her suspicions, but under such circumstances . . . I felt so ridiculously *noble*. Soon after that the communists were defeated. In September '45 Maria left Greece and returned to New York. Alone. Completely alone. The bill, please.'

Cora insisted on paying her share and was rather taken aback when Nagy agreed without protest. As if there was no scope for discussion. Strange. On the other hand . . .

Outside the restaurant both carefully avoided suggesting a particular direction. The last streak of brightness was just leaving the sky. The area was sandwiched between the business and harbour districts and not particularly idyllic.

'Do you have to go home now? No? Won't your husband be worried? No?'

Cora's answer was a terse gesture. Without saying he was heading anywhere specific, Nagy wandered off down the street. He's mad! Completely round the bend! So why do I have this feeling I'm safe with him? She looked for an explanation. One of the more rational ones was: he wouldn't dream of harming me before he's finished telling his story. Logical, wasn't it? When you're dealing with raving lunatics logic isn't always the best guide.

'I like going for walks in the evening. I watch car accidents or buy the *Watchtower* from a Jehova's Witness. Seriously, I get a fiendish pleasure from that. Sometimes. And what about you? What about when you've got your detached house with its electric perimeter fence, what'll you do then?'

'When I've got a detached house? How do you – I mean, what makes you think that's what I want?'

Nagy waved his hand, implying serendipity. 'We don't have to talk about me all the time.'

'Oh yes we do.'

'It's nice of you to go to so much trouble. Giving up your free time for me.'

Cora managed to click her tongue with a gracious shrug of the shoulders, as if to say, 'Think nothing of it', but felt a fraud.

They had come to a dimly lit district which would have been the subject of a tourist warning if there hadn't been too many of them in the city anyway. The streets were getting narrow and filthy. Holes in the road that could break a car in two. Depressing square blocks of council housing and damp rot. The moonlight turned on its heel the moment it touched the tops of the buildings. Each street-lamp was so far away from the next it must have felt completely alone in the world.

'Not particularly salubrious here, is it? We could go down to the sea. I like staring out at the sea, at night; I listen to the song of the spirits as they flutter like dragonflies above the surface of the water . . .'

Cora felt the touch of his sonorous voice with its slight vibrato on her eyelashes, her nostrils, the tips of her breasts and on the back of her neck as she walked in front of him down the narrow alleyway. She would have liked to hang on his lips in a more literal sense. Her self-discipline vanished, giving way to uninhibited lust. She longed to have his fingers, those delicate, slender fingers, on her neck, in her mouth. Sometimes her medical professionalism made a desperate all-out attack and managed to break through. Then she would shake her head, which did nothing to change what was going on inside it. She felt like a woman possessed, and the feeling wasn't an unpleasant one.

Cora had never had sex with patients, unless you count the times, which did occur, when patients started to masturbate before her very eyes and she did nothing to stop them, just watched, unmoved, and let the exhibitionism run its course.

Nagy started talking about the musical box. Had she installed it in its rightful place beside her pillow? 'Installed it in its rightful place beside her pillow.' Sometimes he was like a little boy who had read too many classics, and the wrong ones at that. Cora answered that the music box was fine, the tune very beautiful. He probably wanted to hear a word of thanks from her. Cora refused to do him the favour, though she really couldn't say why. Out of fear he might take it into his head to repeat the exploit? With somewhat more serious consequences this time? Probably. Then he asked an odd question. How was she going to keep the musical-box princess's tutu white, protect it from sunshine, dust and yellowing? It sounded ridiculous. Or profoundly symbolic. Did it contain a hidden reproach? She could think of no better response than to ask him what he would recommend.

'A mild detergent.'

Bucharest (dpa): A 35-year-old Rumanian suffocated on a baby's dummy last weekend. As reported in the Rumanian press on Monday, his 3-month-old son's dummy had fallen on the ground. The father put it into his mouth to 'clean' it, but must have breathed in so strongly as he did that the dummy slipped down into his throat and got stuck there.

A green space appeared, a tiny hummock in the middle of a crossing with two poplars and a park bench on the top. The bench had graffiti sprayed all over it, red and blue tags with which someone was trying to prove their existence. Nagy headed straight for it, sat down and pointed into the distance. Between the houses a patch of ocean could be seen. Garlands of light like a scattering of gold, above it the outlines of gigantic cranes. Pretty.

'Maria's ashes are floating around out there. In a very diluted concentration. Less than a millionth of a gram per cubic metre of water. But it's not quantity that counts. No.'

'I think you're afraid of women.'

'You do?'

'And you try to conceal it with all these bizarre constructs.'

'That's just the kind of diagnosis you get when doctors are baffled. They take refuge in the first plausible explanation they come across so that they're not completely groping in the dark. You're adopting a pose of knowing superiority, humanising me in a most primitive fashion, which is an insult to both our intelligence.'

Cora leant back, inwardly relieved that Nagy did not want to be cured, or at least did not demand a cure too insistently.

Her search for a therapeutic strategy gave way to a sense of pleasure, the kind you feel sitting in the cinema with the rest of the world shut out. She saw patient N. as an actor who had spent a long time rehearsing to himself, or in front of a mirror, and was now finally appearing before an audience. He talked himself into a trance, puffed himself up, kept on reformulating his lines. But if anything happened to disconcert him, made him forget his role, he tumbled into a void, since his real self no longer seemed to exist. Nagy had no biography. If he did, he had misplaced it and would remember where it was only under extreme pressure. Cora saw no reason to put him under such pressure. Or rather had no desire to.

'You managed to get over the two suicides, then?' The question hit her like a slap across the face.

'I'm sorry?' Cora pulled herself together. How on earth had he found out about them?

'Your two patients. Isn't that right?'

'Wherever you got it from, I think you have a cheek to mention them.'

'Oh, but I was very impressed. I didn't mean to hurt your feelings. Please forgive me.'

Cora nodded and rummaged round in her bag for a cigarette, then leant forward over the flame in Nagy's hand. First thing tomorrow she'd hand the case over to a colleague. It really was high time. What do I think I've been doing? Why have I let it go this far?

A delivery truck, going much too fast, turned into the crossroads with a squeal of tyres. On the open back five youths were sitting with a portable radio blasting out hip-hop music.

'What a disgusting racket!' Nagy shot up and shouted after the disappearing van. Cora stood up too and tugged at his sleeve. How could he risk getting into a fight when he was with her? What if the youths had heard him?

'Let's find a taxi. I'd like to go home now.'

This time Cora decided which direction to take, even though she had no idea which square of the city map they were on at the moment. A5? G7? Get away from the docks, that was the main thing. They were bound to get back to lighted shop windows eventually. Nagy strode along beside her, his coat collar turned up. What was wrong? he asked. Was she angry about something? The night was still young and it was warm. Somewhere in the distance the silence was ripped apart by an immense crash, an eruption of metal, a second of pure noise.

There was nothing wrong and she had had a very nice evening. Not, she added, quite as warm as he claimed though, but anyway, didn't he have to go to work in the morning?

'You're not asking that seriously are you?'

Cora did not answer. She had lost that feeling of security. It might have had something to do with the surroundings. The empty windows of an unsuccessful speculative investment grinned at them out of the darkness, beside it an expanse of rubble and torn-down fencing. Rubbish everywhere. Doubtless rats too. Cora marched straight across this stony waste, grimly sticking to the direction in which she assumed the city centre lay. When Nagy stopped then headed off towards some unidentifiable building that stood to one side she snorted with rage.

'Hey! You're not going to leave me by myself, are you?'

'No. What makes you think that? But there's a door open here. I'd like to see what's inside.' Nagy half opened the ten-foot-high door and disappeared. Cora let out a scream of fury and followed him. It was ages since she had seen an underground station, a bus-stop or any other sign of advanced civilisation. The building turned out to be a gymnasium with parquet flooring. A few pieces of apparatus were lying around, a vaulting horse, its leather all torn, a horizontal bar and two medicine balls with their stuffing hanging out.

The building had clearly been condemned, only for some inexplicable reason the demolition had been postponed for decades. The strange thing was that some of the ceiling lamps were still working, and were on, even at this late hour. In an alcove was a pile of rubber mats with worn leather corners. The nets of the basketball baskets were all frayed. There was a smell of stale sweat, wood and rot.

Nagy, his arms crossed, looked round.

Behind the rubber mats something stirred. There was some giggling, then a young Rasta appeared. Hands on hips, he asked what they thought they were looking at. His girl-friend, barely sixteen, gave a spaced-out laugh, emerged from the alcove and started to dance like a slow-motion dervish. There was a strange glow about her. The Rasta's yapping became more aggressive. He pulled out a knife and adopted a number of threatening postures. Nagy drew his revolver. The Rasta stuck his knife back in his trouser pocket, took his girl-friend by the hand and the pair of them disappeared through the other door. The lights went out. A fat, yellow, greasy moon appeared in one of the tilting windows.

'You've really got . . .? Is it real?'
   'What do you think?'
   'I want to get away from here. Quickly!'
   'Okay, okay. Calm down . . .'
   'DON'T YOU TAKE THAT TONE WITH ME!'

8

Robert Dulz's hobby wasn't as unusual as you might think. He collected stories about strange deaths that he cut out of newspapers and magazines and stuck into large scrapbooks. The hour between ten and eleven in the morning, after Cora had left the house, was reserved for this activity. If, on any particular day, there were no new reports to cut out, he would spend the time cataloguing his material and ordering it thematically. His collection of *curiosa* was divided into: accidents; illness; victims of military actions; executions; suicides; murders; attempted murders. Each section was further subdivided according to date, motivation, cultural and ethnic background.

Eventually, Robert hoped, he would have enough material to publish a comprehensive reader on death. A series of short chapters with amusing and gruesome anecdotes, but nothing that was merely disgusting, nothing that wasn't suitable for reading in bed. He even believed he might have a best-seller on his hands, and was occasionally haunted by the fear that someone else might beat him to it with a similar project. Robert used to read his latest discovery out to his wife at dinner sometimes. Cora's response had always been, 'What a topic for the dinner table!' and a nauseated look. In the long run such a response has a discouraging effect, so Robert now kept his scrapbooks locked away in his desk and made no more attempts to interest his wife in his hobby.

And this morning's find had been such a magnificent specimen!

Tokyo: In Japan bowing is considered a token of respect. Now, however, there are more and more calls for it to be abandoned. The reason? When people greet each other in a crowd the result is often a clash of heads. Over the last five years it has been the cause of 24 deaths in Tokyo alone.

Robert was over the moon.

WEEK 2

'Haven't you finished typing it up yet?'

Tammie was just doing the last sentence. Her typing wasn't that quick.

Cora Dulz had spent three days wrestling with her professional conscience; three days deciding not to hand over the N. file after all. A team of advocates inside her brain, specialists in self-justification, found arguments to counter every objection.

There was not another patient on her list with such a well-developed delusion. True, there was that painter who suffered from severe depression. A sad story. When taken back under hypnosis he had discovered he had been Adolf Hitler in his previous existence. And there were patients who heard voices, some who could constantly smell a non-existent odour of decay, others for whom everything tasted too salty or of their mother's milk. There were also patients who suffered from delusions in their visual perception, claimed they could see a heavenly crimson light along the horizon in the evenings or extraterrestrials on television who, disguised as newsreaders, were entangling the whole world in a web of biased reports. Compared with Nagy they were all boring, childish illnesses.

But there were to be no more conversations outside her consulting rooms. And her erotic affinity with him, which had impeded the treatment up to now, had to be repressed, suppressed once and for all. This excessively negative self-image simply cried out to be captured for posterity. The tape recordings would give Cora a double-check on herself, compel her to deal with the case openly. (The Open Case, sounded like a trendy wine bar in the district where the lawyers all had their offices.)

Cora Dulz was satisfied. Her mask of professional objectivity had not slipped once during the whole session. All she had to do was to let the patient keep on talking, that was it. Talking until he skewered himself on the contradictions between delusion and reality. Until he realised the paradoxical nature of his construct.

Cora took the typed pages out of the file and signed and dated them. Only the top half of each page was written on, leaving plenty of room for footnotes.

8 September 4–4.45 pm

N: Maria was out of luck in America. Her Athens triumph meant nothing there. She spent her time running all round the States, from one agent to another, from one director to another. The only decent offer was a Butterfly at the Met. The one role she refused to consider! She rejected it. After months of humiliating begging! That impressed me. It would have been embarrassing to see the role of a sixteen-year-old Japanese girl so generously filled. Maria was well aware of that. As far as management was concerned, however, she was less discerning. Entrusted her affairs to a self-made agent, Bagarozy, an unreliable character full of fancy ideas. He wanted to put on a self-financed *Turandot* with Maria in the title role. The project collapsed, ended in total bankruptcy. A bitter experience that was a lesson to her.[1] Of course, I could have pulled out all the stops, helped Maria, accelerated her career. I did nothing. Nothing at all.[2] For ten years I just watched and listened. Maria was so ambitious. A characteristic I don't value all that highly myself. Every set-back merely doubled her determination. And how I enjoyed it when she wept tears of despair. Oh yes! I hate effortless triumphs. I knew what satisfaction lay in store for Maria. At the moment, though, things looked quite different. No engagements, no success, not even compensation in her sex-life. No lover, no affairs, nothing. All her energy went into her work. And no one wanted to hear the electrically charged voice, not

[1] Sounds as if he's just regurgitating some biography he learnt by heart.
[2] Aha! He admits it himself!

beautiful in the traditional sense, that was the result! Beaten but not bowed, Maria gave up the plan of making her breakthrough in America and accepted an offer from Italy. *La Gioconda* in the Arena di Verona. Not a classy venue, not the Met, La Scala or Covent Garden. But it did give her the chance of singing every night in front of 25,000 people. In Italy, the home of opera. Maria liked Italy. She was treated like a prima donna there or, to put it more precisely, there was a rich industrialist who managed very convincingly to give her the feeling she was a prima donna, a genius. Convincingly and adoringly. His name was Meneghini. He was fifty-three years old, fat and unprepossessing. He doted on Maria, devoted his life to her, did everything for her, drove her around, paid for her luxurious life-style, sat whole nights through at her bedside when she was ill. Very touching, don't you think? I put no obstructions in his way. On the contrary. There had to be someone in Maria's life, and I much preferred a man like that to some tone-deaf, handsome young gigolo, I would be furious with all the time.

D: You said 'furious with'. Don't you mean 'jealous of?'

N: Only in a different sense from the most obvious. I didn't desire Maria physically. Not at all! Especially at that time. It's hundreds of years since I last slept with a woman.

D: Hundreds of years?[3]

N: It's tedious.

D: Really?

N: I'm being completely honest with you.

D: Could it be that you despise women?

N: Nonsense! Half of my clientele consists of women.

D: Why is the Devil a man? Can you explain that to me?

N: Why should *I* explain that?[4] You're wasting my money. *You're* the one who should be answering that question. I

[3] I should have formulated my question more precisely. 'When was the last time?' for example. Or, 'With whom?'

[4] Presumably a feigned outburst.

used to go around with goat's feet! With horns sticking out of my head! And no one bothered to explain the significance of that to me.[5]

D: I understand. You're just an image, a projection of people's feelings.

N: If you like.

D: Is God a man?

N: If he was, women would be born wearing high heels. No, seriously, your question's meaningless.

D: Then I withdraw it.

N: D'you know something? When God and I were still addicted to our little bets, for the odd soul or two, we used to fight like anything! Tooth and nail! As if the world might go up in flames, depending on the result, or at least the odd continent.

D: Was that a long time ago?

N: The old days. Those *were* the days! People would call me up, secretly, I would arrive at midnight, they would offer me a soul for sale, I'd give the soul the once-over and name a price. Most were a bit disappointed at first, but soon realised they should be glad to get anything at all for a filthy black thing like that. The artists were the best! They really took themselves seriously!

D: What did you do with the souls?

N: Chucked them away. Do I have to keep everything?

D: And Hell? What's with Hell?

N: Hell? What does that mean to you? Brueghel? A kind of home video where I amuse myself watching the torments of the damned? How long do you think that would keep me amused? Clichés!

D: Hmmm . . .

N: For example the idea I could just enter a person, like going into a drive-in Macdonalds, and take possession of him is a very childish notion. I can only manage that when my 'host' expressly permits it, when he opens

---

[5] Very neat! But I shouldn't be admiring these rhetorical sidesteps, I should be destroying them.

himself up to me, so to speak, and asks me in. Even that's not all it's cracked up to be. I have never come across a human being I've been able to stand being inside for more than a few minutes. It's so cramped. If you must know, I quickly develop claustrophobia inside someone else. What are you grinning at?[6]

D: Perhaps it would be better if we got back to Maria?

N: That's the odd thing about you. Sometimes you're full of curiosity, then at others . . .

D: What happened in Verona?

N: In Verona? Did something happen there? What? Nothing happened. One critic wrote that it would be difficult to tell the difference between Callas's legs and the elephant's. The audience was indifferent. At best lukewarm. I couldn't understand it. I couldn't care, either. *I* could hear her. That was enough. Then she went to Venice, sang Wagner. Isolde. Didn't really suit her voice. Teatro La Fenice. At last she was famous. At last she had the confirmation she needed. The first storms of applause that built up into hurricanes. I enjoyed that too. In my eyes she was still the gawky, spotty young girl who was suspicious of all applause precisely because that was what she had been hoping for and working towards. Success that stirs up more self-doubt than all the earlier rejection – that appeals to my sense of drama. It's always effective. Everything was effective. And her fame grew. She got better and better. Better than even I had anticipated. It was a voice you could lose yourself in, as in one of the eleusinian mysteries. And her industry did not flag at all. As far as her physical needs were concerned, Meneghini was no real distraction. Maria was a star. A great star. The best. One critic said she was divine. *La Divina*! Many followed suit. Divine! Horrible word. A marketing slogan with a claim to eternity! Maria wasn't divine. She was a very *human* person, full of suppressed lust, liable to fits of violent temper, vain and miserly, weighed down with complexes,

[6] I shook my head, bit my lip. Otherwise self-control good.

63

greedy for applause.[7] Lusted after cries of 'Bravo!' like a vampire after blood. Larger and larger doses were necessary. Sometimes, when the audience went wild, she felt she was in heaven. It wasn't heaven. I knew that. She wanted to be a star, the brightest of all, the one at the zenith. And was consumed in her own fire. Some roles she learnt in weeks, others in a few days. She rescued virtuoso, if musically uninteresting operas from oblivion; forgotten works, which had not been performed for decades for lack of a singer capable of breathing life into them, the life which justified performance. Maria loved such finds. She knew very well that it would be a long time before another singer would come who could make a spellbinding evening of *Anna Bolena, La Vestale* or *Alceste*. As I said, she was greedy. Not for money. Her pursuit of higher and higher fees was simply an expression of her need for recognition; self-doubt which seeks louder and louder applause, only to grow along with the applause. And if the enthusiastic crowd contained just *one* idiot who booed – and there were some, even in those early days – the recognition meant nothing to her. History is a heartless taskmaster who throws mediocrities on the garbage heap. Just think how many sopranos, who had known glittering success, now found that the presence of Maria consigned them to the ranks of the merely average. The intensity of love is quickly matched by an even greater intensity of hatred. Often I felt so sorry for her I could have cried with, I won't say *happiness*, but *emotion*.

D: Why didn't you do something?

N: It had to be! The last thing I wanted in Maria was a self-satisfied heroine. So much depended on her! The torch had to burn. Burn! And there was so much in Maria to fuel the flames! Oh dear, I have the feeling I'm talking and talking while you would rather be asking questions like did I masturbate too much during puberty?

D: How would you define 'too much'?

[7] Does he identify with these qualities himself?

N:[8] Something incredible happened. Is there still time?[9]

D: Sure.

N: She began to starve herself. A remarkable exercise of will-power, as if she wanted to disappear. Stopped eating chocolates, even gave up her beloved macaroni with eggs and sheep's cheese. Fourteen stones she weighed, and now, within a few months, she was down to almost half of her old self, was slim, with elfin looks, the face of a mythological beauty, something between Artemis and Pallas Athene.

And me? What did I do? Dressed up as a doctor and spread the rumour she'd had a tape-worm implanted in her bowels. Is there anything worse one could do to a woman? The rumour's still doing the rounds today. Fiendish, don't you think? A disgusting monster? But I needed it. Needed it there and then. Why else would I exist?

My admiration, the way I shared in everything she did, the way I depended on her . . . all that changed, was transformed into an unspeakable longing, a painful need to be close to her . . .

D: Love?

N: A half-baked concept.

D: Love.

N: Yes, dammit, yes! Maria was so beautiful. She was famous. Now she became the best-known woman in the world. Just listening to her wasn't enough any longer. Don't misunderstand me.[10] She was a synthesis of all the arts, freed of all imperfections, and she aroused and annoyed me. I had to share in it! Somehow or other! I had to speak to her, whisper words in her ear, urge her on to good and evil. For too long I had listened, just listened.

---

[8] Fairly long pause, patient unsure of himself, staring right across the room; then regained concentration.

[9] Patient stood up, raised both arms, sighed, sat down, then spoke more quietly.

[10] In a whisper, very intensely.

And then, one evening I became aware of something. It was . . . February '57. *Norma* at Covent Garden, a splendid house. I took my seat and leafed through the programme, looked round at the packed boxes, saw the glitter, smelled the women's perfume . . .

Just picture it: a large, brightly lit opera house full of music-starved ears, which seem to have been waiting in their seats for months. The women so elegant, the men so sophisticated! After only the second bell silence reigns, even the little pack of hostile claqueurs has gone quiet. The chandelier is drawn up, the lights go out. The conductor is greeted with waves of applause much more rapturous than is called for by his reputation. The audience is taking advantage of their last opportunity to relax the tension. The overture. Seems to drag. The curtains open. At last! Heads appear in the boxes, lots of them, leaning right out over the balustrade: Maria, in the middle of the stage, in the middle of the light. Her long white dress. Her first note. It's an act of worship – only now do I realise it! – an act of divine worship, goddammit! I start to go deaf, to shrivel up. This celebration is not for me. The miracle mocks me. Beauty disdains me cruelly.

Impossible to stay, impossible to get up and leave. The situation repeated itself hundreds of times. I suffered and I was enthralled; I hated her and loved her, wished myself dead, wished her dead. Could never make up my mind which.

Her most magnificent performance, and the most depressing for me, was in the ancient theatre in Epidaurus, where she played Medea, where she *was* Medea, a Greek myth returned to its place of origin, as if Euripides had died but yesterday.

In her moments of triumph – triumphs which a single individual ought not to enjoy – I did some nasty things to her, horrible things, even stupid things. Threw radishes onto the stage when it was raining roses. And Maria, shortsighted as she was, picked them up and, only recognising what they were too late, pressed the radishes to her breast with a weary smile, and reaped even greater applause for her magnanimity. But afterwards, in the dressing-room, she cried to think that someone could be so spiteful to her. At times like that what would I have not given to be able to comfort her. How often did I attempt to become her friend, her confidant.

The more I worshipped her, the greater my desire to wound her, to torment her, to spoil her enjoyment of life. Not because she rejected me. On the contrary, I was fascinated by the almost animal instinct with which she sniffed out my every disguise and avoided me.

D: If you really are the Devil, don't you have powers which would prove to me you're not just pretending?[11]

N: Oh come on! Haven't I come to you? Haven't I revealed myself? Is there the slightest suggestion I haven't been completely open and honest? Do you know of anyone else who claims to be me?

D: One up to you.

N: My power is bound to contracts. It only comes into effect when my presence is expressly requested.[12] I was often close to Maria without her knowing. Watched her bathing in bathrooms of marble and gold, worthy of some oriental nabob. But even then, she still only bathed in water. Not a princess out of the Arabian Nights, a woman like many others. As a voyeur such scenes did not arouse me. No, I didn't want to sleep with her. I wanted companionship, friendship, affection, closeness; I wanted to feel what was going on inside her. If someone was determined to see it in a negative light, they could say I was doing it all just to gain prestige. I wanted her to recognise me, to acknowledge me, to respect me, ask my advice, cry on my shoulder, just be herself with me.

[11] Much too direct. Endangers the trust between us. More subtlety next time.
[12] Who does he have under contract? Ask for examples. Appeal to his vanity!

D: Assuming you'd succeeded, what could you offer her in return?

N: Nothing. Why should I? I'm the Devil, not a sugar daddy.[13] Oh, you know . . . Deep down inside I'm not such a bad chap really, it's just everything's so boring, so mind-blowingly boring. So you play games. And in games there are winners and losers. You human beings have long since realised that. Wouldn't have it any other way.

Is this conversation being recorded?

D: No.

N: It's just that I thought I could hear something. Like a tape running. Are you lying to me?

D: No.[14]

N: Good. Time's up.

(cut)

[13] The patient gave me a positively cocksure look, even emphasised the bizarre logic of his answer with a wink.

[14] Should I have not denied it? It was impossible for the patient to detect the tape, either visually or acoustically. Knowing he was being recorded would only have reinforced his compulsion to play-act.

10

On Wednesday, 9 September Nagy did not appear for his appointment. Nor did he ring up to cancel or arrange a new time. Cora Dulz waited. Each day she extended the journey home, which took four stations on the underground, by getting off at the third, then the second and finally the first station. The no-man's-land between the end of work and dinner gave her a feeling of emptiness and the compulsive urge to fill it. She looked at newspapers in the display cases, posters on hoardings or slabs in the pavement; then at the sun, or a prematurely brown leaf on a tree that was still green.

Cora caught herself accusing Nagy, inwardly furious at so much love wasted on a dead woman. Like pouring water over the sand in front of people dying of thirst.

She had accepted that what had happened, and ought not to happen in her profession, had happened and there was no changing it. It gave her a tingle, a shimmer, like a schoolgirl in love.

Her loneliness. Only in Nagy's presence did it give way to purpose, to joy: was she strong enough to admit that to herself without being completely lost?

Cora needed all her will-power to force herself to wait a whole week for a sign of life from her favourite patient. She asked Tammie three times a day whether he had been in touch. Tammie said no. Tammie was so stupid.

The furniture she had lavished such care on choosing no longer gave Cora any pleasure. It had a tired, worn look and cried out to be exchanged or chopped up for firewood. In three years I'll be forty. The crow's-feet round her eyes nodded heartless agreement. Not one square inch of the mirror had the energy or decency to contradict them. When I decided to marry Robert the prospect of never having to tear my hair over a tax declaration ever again was a not insignificant factor.

Cora began to neglect her patients. Some appointments she simply cancelled, others she got through without exerting herself, simply by pretending to listen and dropping in the odd, 'Really?' or 'Great'. Two cases of minor paranoia, who noticed this and complained about it, she referred to the city psychiatric clinic 'for observation'.

Patients. *Regulars.* No prospect of surprises. People who blame everyone but themselves for their screwed-up lives. Depressives produced by affluence. Bores. Like me.

The amount of dirt housed under the nail of Robert's right ring finger was impossible to ignore. Cora's expression suggested a shadow had darkened the table, or the wing of a fallen angel. Robert's habit of poking around in his food until his fork held a precise combination of meat, potato and asparagus, the scraping noise of the fork and, as the climax of the whole grisly performance, the raising and licking-clean of the plate – how could anyone forget his manners like that just for a few drops of bechamel sauce? And how disgusting of a man to belch audibly and then ask his wife for a glass of Fernet Branca as *his stomach was hissing and gurgling*.

This is the man, thought Cora, who's had oral sex with you. Several times.

In the evening she sat out in the garden until it got dark, framed by a Chinese basket chair which made her look small and fragile.

What have I done wrong? Why has Nagy broken off the treatment? Was I *too* aloof? Too disbelieving? Did Nagy no longer feel at ease in his other world?

'Cora!? D'you want to watch the film?'
'Leave me in peace.'
The tomcats padded along the hedge and circled round their feeding bowls, sniffing. There was food out for them. Another satisfactory evening. Tomorrow there'd be tuna, then beef, then game. Several weeks' supply of tins were piled up in the cupboard, already arranged in the correct order.

'Problems?'

Robert leant down and put a pullover round Cora's shoulders. She flung it off onto the lawn. Immediately regretted it, but refused to get up and bend down.

Her no longer beloved in the twilight. Crying or sweating? Dripping, anyway.

Woman murdered with axe in cathedral

Hamburg (rtr): During early mass in St. Mary's in Hamburg on Wednesday a 42-year-old woman murdered an old-age pensioner with an axe.

The woman, who was arrested while still in the church, was clearly mentally disturbed. According to the police, she believed her victim was possessed by the devil. First of all she sprinkled the 72-year-old woman, who was sitting in front of her, with holy water, then struck her with a 15-inch axe, inflicting serious injuries from which her victim later died in hospital. At the time of the attack there were some 15 worshippers attending the morning service.

The Portuguese priest who was celebrating mass did not notice the incident, a church spokesman said. After her arrest the woman claimed she had been preparing for the deed for eighteen months and now felt a great sense of relief.

WEEK 3

11

WEDNESDAY

By the seventh day the waiting had become unbearable and Cora set out to find her lost patient. It turned out that the address on the patient registration form was an invention, that there was no such place as Mark Chapman Street in the city. The telephone number Nagy had written down was equally a figment of his imagination.

Cora marched up to the porter's lodge at Pullam's Department Store. She was relieved to see there the corpulent man in uniform who had been on duty a fortnight ago. And he appeared to remember her, as his suggestive grin indicated all too clearly. Stanislaus Nagy? Didn't work here any more, had been given notice, or had given in his notice, the bosses would know the details. His address? Could be it was still in the ledger, but with the data protection act . . . If it was that important, she could ask the personnel manager, tomorrow morning, at the moment . . . Cora slipped a bank-note under the glass. The fat man raised his index finger and then his middle finger. He wasn't being insulting, it just meant two.

A high-rise mass grave made of reinforced concrete on the edge of the docks area. The panel alongside the bell buttons contained a good eighty names, many written by hand, faded, hardly legible or derived from a foreign alphabet. Nagy lived fairly high up, she had to guess at the storey since there were no numbers beside the names. The outside door was not locked, so Cora went in. Dim neon lighting. Anonymity expressed in architecture. Endless corridors in non-colours, one door the same as the next, each one presumably opening onto the same tiny bedsit with cooking facilities and minimal balcony, on which the occupants could stand and stare at the twin tower block opposite.

A faint smell of urine put Cora off using the lift. She climbed the stairs and started looking when she reached the sixth floor. One long corridor to the left, one long corridor to the right. With each floor the corridors seemed to get longer and eerier. Now and then she heard screaming, a dull thud that sounded like a head landing on carpet, music with a thumping bass. Then silence again. In some of the corridors the lighting wasn't working, but Cora continued her search with the aid of her cigarette lighter, the flame turned down as far as possible without letting it go out. There were doors with nothing, not even a single initial, to indicate who lived there. Nagy, perhaps? She swore and complained softly to herself. Why is there no one here to ask? At this hour people should be coming home from work. Or does nobody here work? Lazy sods!

Cora cursed and swore, immediately regretted the expletives and took them back; but they did help keep her spirits up.

At last! Eighth floor, left wing, next to last door: *Nagy*. Blue ink on an ex-white ground. And if he wasn't in? Cora wondered what message she should leave. Please call this number? What nonsense!

She knocked. She could have rung, down at the entrance, there was an entryphone, but her fear of being turned away had made her plump for direct confrontation. She knocked again. And again.

'Yes?'

'Cora Dulz.'

A moment's pause.

'It's open.'

The flat looked grotty. Odd pieces of crockery mixed up with charity-shop buys. Messily torn-out newspaper articles pinned to the walls. Pillows squashed and stained, the bed-clothes crumpled up into a heap, probably pushed down to the end of the bed by Nagy because of the heat. Piles of tinned food on the shelves either side of the cooker. Cora looked for photographs of the adored diva. There was nothing that reflected his passion, not even books. And his stereo system looked cheap and small. The room was so untidy you didn't notice how bare it was. Cora stared in appalled fascination at the wall-to-wall carpeting that resembled nothing so much as the skin of an old cat with a bad case of scabies. Nothing in the room anyone would call beautiful or cosy, nothing the occupant had ever taken any trouble over. Apart from the bed, on which Nagy was sitting with his legs drawn up, the only seat appeared to be a reddish-brown leather armchair splitting open at the seams. The light from the low-watt bulb on the ceiling was further dimmed by a pale red globe that reminded Cora of the seventies, of her childhood. The curtains over the only window were drawn almost right across. The Armani suit was hanging on a coat-hanger, the coat-hanger from the top knob of the chest of drawers. On the bedside cabinet were two beer bottles, one empty, the other almost. Nagy was smoking. He was wearing a T-shirt and jeans and had bare feet. His whole posture seemed somehow twisted and sad. Cora did not have the impression her visit was welcome.

'Doctor Dulz . . .' Nagy spoke her name softly, as if he were simply stating a fact. His voice was clear, with no trace of drunkenness. Each time he took a deep breath he exhaled audibly through his nose. Cora stayed by the door and kept on looking down at the carpet, as if there were a swamp full of bloodthirsty leeches in front of her.

'This is where you live?'

'Well, I'm just a poor devil.'

'You didn't turn up for your appointment.'

'I didn't? Sorry.' Fifteen seconds silence.

'I was worried.'

'You were? That's nice.' He seemed to have no desire to talk. Cora felt she had to act in a more decisive manner. In no way should she apologise for her presence here; on the contrary, it was Nagy who had the explaining to do.

'What happened?' She took two steps into the room, and in so doing discovered a strange piece of furniture in the far right-hand corner, between the balcony door and the chest of drawers. A deep-freeze. A huge deep-freeze, more suited to a hotel kitchen than this claustrophobic toilet with living-space. On top of it was an eighteen-inch mountain of candle wax, three colours of candle wax mingled together: red, black, blue. Scraps of wick could be seen everywhere inside the dribbled mass, or sticking out like bristles. On the summit three candles were burning, slowly losing their cylindrical shape and melting into the wax massif. There was something very appealing about it.

Why had she come today of all days? he asked. Did she know what day it was? The 16th of September. The anniversary of Maria's death. At this time of the year he suffered from melancholy and avoided the company of human beings.

Cora expressed her condolences, unintentionally sounding sarcastic, and asked whether she ought to leave. Would he be coming to the practice tomorrow? she added.

Nagy got down off the bed, staggered over to the stereo system and inserted a cassette. Wild music poured out, from which a female voice emerged singing something like 'Holotoho', dozens of times. Was she extolling a Japanese prince?

Cora had never been able to stand opera and therefore never listened to any. The sound of a symphony orchestra, she thought, was not unpleasant, but singing over it, shrill and piercing . . . to think there were people who made a religion of it . . .

'Fantastic, isn't it? Maria as the Valkyrie, '49, in Venice.'

'Great. Should we agree on a time?'

'Why?'

'I think you need help.'

Nagy got up, rummaged in a drawer, took out a shirt and went into the bathroom. The door was left open a crack, through which came the sound of a shower.

'TO BE HONEST, I DON'T KNOW HOW I'M GOING TO PAY YOU.'

'IN YOUR CASE YOUR MEDICAL INSURANCE WILL PAY.'

'I HAVEN'T GOT ANY MEDICAL INSURANCE.'

'EVERY PERSON HAS MEDICAL INSURANCE.'

'WHY TALK ABOUT THESE THINGS? DO YOU LIKE CHAMPAGNE?'

'VERY MUCH.'
'HOW ABOUT BUYING SOME FOR US?'

Haze was settling over the late afternoon, rendering it soft and slow. Striped awnings above the shop windows gave a pretence of Mediterranean chic. With Cora's money Nagy had bought a cooled bottle of Veuve Cliquot at the delicatessen. Carrying the bottle and two paper cups, the pair of them made their way to the central park, spread a newspaper on the grass and sat down in the sun, which had just reached the tips of the chestnut trees The hills were charging themselves with dramatic light. It was beautiful, peaceful and cheap. Cora asked herself why she hadn't sat here more often.

'Perhaps the reason I stopped coming to see you was that my story is about to get embarrassing.'

'In my profession you get used to all sorts of things.'

Can one say of a face that it strikes a pose? Confronted with the expression on Nagy's features, the answer would have to be yes.

'As I said before, I wanted to be close to Maria. But whatever disguise I assumed, she sensed me. No idea why. Perhaps she really had some kind of inner eye, though my suspicion falls on the big prompter in the sky. But that's just by the way. I've told you I find it difficult to take possession of a human being. It's different with animals. With them it's relatively simple. Maria had a poodle that she took everywhere with her, a black poodle – how appropriate! – of which she was very fond. She called it *Toy*.' he paused. His lips grew thin, his eyes glassy.

'Toy. A stupid little beast. Easy to occupy. I often borrowed that dog. Just pulled him on like a glove, walked on all fours and wore a collar. That's how desperate I was to have Maria's fingers fondling me . . .'

'Lovely story!' Cora was touched. Any more and the corners of her eyes would have been glistening with moistness. Nagy smiled, as if amused at himself. Then he pulled something out of his jacket pocket.

'There's a picture of Maria, God and me. Do you know it? No? There. The *black* poodle, that's me.'

The faded newspaper cutting had been stuck onto clear film. Cora didn't know whether to laugh or cry, and it was only the fact that each impulse cancelled the other out that allowed her to appear outwardly calm.

'I have never been close to her, except as a dog. In that form she fondled me, liked me and didn't recognise me. I felt rather stupid clutched in her arm, but I also felt wonderful . . .' His smile evaporated. 'No! For a moment it was wonderful, just for a moment. Then it was horrible. A pooch with a curly black mane and a docked tail! That wasn't me! It was a sham! So bogus! Completely lacking in dignity or style, like this paper cup.' He crushed it in his hand. 'How could I stoop so low?! I hated myself for it and my hatred rebounded on Maria. I tormented her and all the time I was tormenting myself. I was my own little voodoo doll. There aren't enough words to talk my pain away, to make another person feel it, feel the cold I felt. I wanted Maria to know, to sense, to have some inkling at least that I existed, that I was engaged in a struggle for her. Just once I wanted her to hold *me* in her arm the way she was holding that dog, just once to stroke me the way she stroked that guaranteed tick-free poodle fur!'

Nagy jumped up and ran down the mound, straight through the clematis bushes towards the ring road. Cora had difficulty catching up with him.

'What's the matter?'

'I can't stand it in this park any more. Maria brought me out here for walkies once. Do you see that tree there?' He pointed somewhere behind him. 'I cocked a leg against that tree.'

Cora wanted to laugh out loud. Her stomach muscles were getting sore from all the laughter she was having to force back down.

More! she thought, completely without pity, just greedy for more entertainment. Tell me more. Be what you want to be. Amuse me. The half bottle of Veuve Cliquot stood abandoned on the top of the mound. Sinister figures crept towards it, argued over it.

Nagy crossed the four lane highway, slowed down then stopped, as if he had lost all sense of where he was, where he was going.

'I tormented Maria. Tormented her and loved her. And caused her downfall.'

'Why do you burden yourself with all this guilt? What compels you to do it? Why are you making all this up?'

Nagy looked at her in astonishment, rubbing his right earlobe. The twilight had reached a strange tone, somewhere between ochre and an orangey blue, impossible to name, which was rapidly being sucked in by the darkness. The brick chimneys of the old town stood out like the silhouettes of churches or peel towers, menacing and romantic. The street lamps flickered into life. The little cafes, of which there was an abundance in this area, switched on their neon signs. For reasons of cost, the modest little water jet in the fountain detumesced completely.

Nagy stayed silent for a long time, then pushed himself away from the wall he was leaning against and set off walking, without bothering whether Cora was following him or not. Was he offended? she asked. A shake of the head. Did he really think she could believe his story, just like that? Especially, she added in an almost apologetic rider, as she thought of herself as a scientist, an enlightened person. Nagy stopped briefly, muttering that he was used to disbelief, it wasn't her *fault*, but it was most definitely *her* problem, he didn't have to prove himself to anyone. Cora, who had long since given up following therapeutic guidelines, admitted that there were doubtless more aeroplanes flying between heaven and earth than were dreamt of in Newton's philosophy.

Nagy, eyes screwed up, was staring at the gutter. Then he turned up his coat collar.

What's he thinking about? Is he plunging back into his imaginary world, getting stuck in it? It's one of those moments when I'd just love to show him some affection. There's a demonic beauty about him when he does his sufferer act. When things are going on inside him and the words come out with a hiss.

'As a woman Maria was completely unsatisfied. But she sublimated it in a very meaningful way. Then along came Onassis. How I hated him! But there was nothing I could do. She loved him. And he gave it to her. He was fiendishly good in bed.'

I want him to tear my blouse off, be rough with me, stick his hand up my skirt, take me from behind. I want to bite him and claw my nails into his skin, want to have his panting in my ear, to suck the moans from his lips, feel his teeth on my knees, at my neck, in my shoulders, I want him to grab me and treat me like a doll.

Nagy suddenly looked up as if he had been following Cora's thoughts.

'Is there anything you'd like?'

'A coffee wouldn't be bad.'

Tie him to the bed, suck him until he gets a hard-on and then mount it.

'It's Maria's day. I hope you won't take it the wrong way if I suggest we postpone the idea of coffee.'

'Of course not. When will we see each other?'

Nagy gave a weary shrug of the shoulders. 'Oh, we'll see each other . . . Wait! There's one more thing.'

It seemed to her that Nagy's body was losing its three-dimensional quality, becoming shadowy in places, almost transparent. Cora assumed it was one of the standard tricks the twilight plays on the retina.

'You must promise that you won't record our conversations ever again. Ever again.'

'But . . .'

'Please don't lie. I know you're lying. With good reason, from your point of view. But still, promise?'

Cora nodded feebly, still convinced Nagy's suspicion was a shot in the dark. But the conviction with which he expressed it had reached the degree of intensity at which one simply *had* to make concessions to a sick mind. Unless, of course, the treatment were taking place in a secure ward where the patient's freedom of movement was restricted. Interesting idea.

Tbilisi: Surab Dugashvili, a Georgian chess master, died during the national championships after receiving a fatal wound in the right eye from an illegal bishop's move.

His opponent was arrested in the hall where the championships were being held. The tournament committee awarded him the point for the match, although 'with an angry heart'. The decisive factor, the chief referee said, was that Surab D. had not objected to the illegal move and had lost the game 'by exceeding the time limit'.

12

SATURDAY

It was ages since Robert and Cora had been out together. In fact, they had neglected the small intersection of the sets of their friends for months now. So when Cora suggested they attend the opening of an exhibition by an object artist they'd once met briefly, he was somewhat bemused, but couldn't think of any objections.

It was raining. Cora was wearing her most striking dress, the little pink number with the frills. The electronic display board at the roadside was running adverts. A drummer bunny was drumming as it leant over the lifeless figure of the drummer bunnyette, asking in a tone of bitter mourning, *Why has your battery run down already? Why don't you have Duracell?*

Robert was saying he was sick and tired of the kind of advertising that made such a blatant appeal to the emotions when the bunny started ravishing his flat-batteried mate and he realised the information board belonged to the gallery. Fake advertising, i.e. art.

The objects that were being offered for sale were not on stands, they were hanging from the ceiling on nylon threads. There was a swallow-like bird-shape hewn from a brick. And there were completely unhewn bricks with labels indicating which species of bird the artist had transformed into brick. Blackbird, thrush, starling, finch. On a very large brick was written *Eagle or vulture?* which implied a very ambivalent attitude towards capitalism. Could have been meant ironically. Like the price in the catalogue. The artist, amid a besieging army of reviewers, was playing it coy. All he was concerned about, he emphasised, was sex, admiration and money; everything else was dangerous nonsense.

Rooms of sterile brightness. Cora saw faces she knew, said Hi, waved, felt bored stiff. What had she been thinking of, coming here? With Robert in tow? A forcible attempt to take her mind off Nagy? To bring some life back into her marriage, to stop her destructive thoughts from developing any further? An attempt at resistance which, as she could feel, was only speeding matters up.

Robert's not a bad husband. Said his mother. Perhaps there are better husbands but they, as the word implies, are married.

Rotating spotlights. The brick mobiles were moving too.

His mother strongly advised him against marrying me. *I was too much like her.* An insult, certainly. But, when you think about it, directed at whom? At herself? At me? At Robert? At all of us? God rest her soul.

In the largest of the rooms there was a buffet and music. One of the two musicians, the one at the keyboard with folding legs, had brought along some pictures of his own. Fuzzy photographs of television test cards that had been painted over. They had a certain mythic quality. No trace of irony. He placed the pictures round his keyboard, hoping to be discovered. The owner of the gallery insisted he remove his parasitic art, pointing out that the gallery wasn't a flea-market. The saxophonist blew his soulful, doleful notes and kept well out of it.

Soon little groups would form, conversations start up, the inevitable questions be asked. Such as, What's new? No problem, there's always something new. How often had Cora, without thinking, ignored medical confidentiality and fed some social gathering comic stories from her practice. Just so that Robert, that inadequate tax consultant, could spend the whole evening in comfortable silence.

Once you've passed thirty-five you discover, to your surprise, that the world has produced a new generation behind your back. There is a cohort of twenty-year-olds who have been drilled in schools and colleges and are now ready for action. The world goes rolling on, leaving you behind, and you think, Why? Why does it want to go through all that again?

There were countless beautiful women in the world, and many of them were here. The number was growing by the hour. They all had long slim legs. With no insect bites whatsoever.

You're never as young as you were. Maria's dead. Hasn't anything I haven't got.

Robert could be proud of me. Or at least grateful he can be a parasite on the back of my small talk. He's standing over there with Arnold, they're looking across at me. I wonder what Robert is saying, if he's saying anything?

'I have the feeling Cora's been having an affair.'

'Is there anything special about that?'

'To the best of my knowledge, she's never been unfaithful.'

'And you?'

'To the best of her knowledge I've never been unfaithful.'

Arnold's grinning in my direction. How can Robert manage to get anyone to grin, even if only Arnold? Could they possibly be having a laugh at my expense?

I'd like to get drunk and make a scene, like one of those complex characters with tattered nerves you get in old films, those horribly hysterical films nobody can watch today. In my cells there's a gene that's ordering my body to age. If I could switch it off I might live for a hundred thousand years. How about that for the title of a novel? *A hundred thousand years of Robert*.

The little groups formed. What's new with the freaks? Cora knew what her audience wanted and she felt the urge to tell them about patient N., to serve his illness up on a plate as little canapés of lunatic behaviour. It was a great story. With God, who looked old, radishes pretending to be roses, and a dog you could pull on like a glove. A guaranteed laugh, garnished with details like the massive freezer, the mountain of candlewax and the soprano singing Holotoho!

The crucial response came unexpectedly, a mere murmur, a shot from the hip, so to speak.

'The Valkyrie, you say? You mean Brunnhilde?'

The man with the grey walrus moustache. Schwerdtko-Mirov. The one with the reading glasses dangling down over his hand-knitted pullover.

'Could be.'

'Could *not* be.' These restrained know-alls who always wait for a cue before letting off. The ones who've learnt to dispense their knowledge in small doses so that it gives the impression of a fund of learning, but still sounds casual, best of all ever so slightly inebriated, the most underhand form of understatement.

'Maria Callas did sing the role, in Italian, but there's no recording of it. Absolutely not.'

'No? But I heard it with my own ears.'

'Are you sure it was Callas?'

Cora thought for a moment before admitting that classical vocal music was something she was not familiar with, that her ability to discriminate was not very well developed.

'In that case . . .'

For the arrogance of that 'In that case' Cora could have gladly punched Schwerdtko-Mirov on his fat nose.

In the taxi on the way home Robert touched Cora's knee but, since the reaction was cool, pretended it was unintentional. If she was having an affair, okay then. No reason to start thinking of a divorce as long as the non-physical side of their relationship was still functioning. He wouldn't ask any questions.

Outside it was still raining.

At one point they both had the same thought: that it was pleasant to be driven round at night through the rain, looking out of rain-streaked windows, watching the people in the streets. Both thought of telling the driver to do a couple of extra laps. Both remained silent.

Their terraced house was still standing where they'd left it a few hours before. A faithful house.

Robert got into bed and started to leaf through a pile of newspapers. Cora rummaged round in her bedside cabinet, took something out and locked herself in the bathroom. If you held your breath you could hear a gentle, battery-driven humming. Robert didn't take it personally.

Sex while driving – Susan and Malcolm dead

Halifax: Sex while driving cost 41-year-old Malcolm Whitham and his 37-year-old partner Susan Charman their lives.

The couple were returning home from a party in Halifax in the north of England. While still driving Malcolm pulled his trousers down and Susan took off her blouse and bra. Then she bent down over him . . .

Suddenly Malcolm lost control of their 14-year-old Ford Escort on a bend. The car lurched, rammed into a traffic sign then crashed into a wall.

Both died in the crash. Susan broke her neck, Malcolm, a police officer, hit his head against the windscreen.

The couple leave four children aged between 3 and 15. Susan's father, Leonard Charman (70), said, 'I don't understand why they had to do it in the car. Surely they could have waited till they got home.'

13

Among her post on Monday evening Cora found a hand-written letter with no sender's address but signed S. N.

Robert had put it on the living-room table along with the junk mail.

How has Nagy found my address? All in a day's work for a detective I suppose, but I'd still like to know ... My telephone number is ex-directory. There are over seventy Dulzes in the city register, three of them Roberts. And anyway, my husband's first name was never mentioned.

You doubted me. And I was touchy about it. Sorry!

Keep your doubts. They are deeply ingrained, as unalterable as the small print in a contract you can't get out of.

Is that a veiled reference to my wrinkles?

But the way you express them could be a little less crude.

More subtlety next time, please. And your consulting room. It's a dreadful place. Couldn't we meet somewhere else, assuming you are still interested in my case.

> *With best wishes,*
> *S. N.*

Robert wasn't the kind of man to check her correspondence. To ask her who a letter with no sender's address on the outside was from and what it was about. Certainly not the kind of man to steam it open and then seal it again. Robert was not at all a typical man. Didn't even give her cause to keep things secret from him.

'A patient wrote me a letter today.'

'Does it say nice things?'

'I'm wondering how he got hold of my address.'

'Hmm.'

'There's another funny thing about it. He's written, *More subtlety next time.* The context is irrelevant, but those are the very words I used in a footnote to the transcript of his consultation. It's not just any old set phrase, is it? Could it be coincidence?'

'Hmm.'

'And there's a couple of other odd things. He once alluded to the detached house I'd like to have. And he told me straight out our conversation was being taped. He even knew about the two suicides.'

'Suicides?'

'You see, even you don't know.' She told Robert about it, reluctantly, regretting having mentioned the business at all. If you wanted to be surprised by Robert you had to play Scrabble against him. Coincidence, he replied, was capable of anything, though it used its powers less often than one might think. Robert was not only not a typical man, he also had a reflective streak. He went on, as if to open up an even wider world of possibilities, 'There's a *rational* explanation for everything. Whether it's the right one or not.'

14
TUESDAY

'My father came back to the caravan, his shoulders drooping despondently. He'd been for a walk along the beach and lost his wristwatch. And I, little seven-year-old me, leapt up and cried, I'll find it! I dashed down to the sea and, bending down low, scoured a mile of sand before I suddenly found a middle-aged woman standing in front of me. Could this be what you're looking for? My father's watch was gleaming in her hand! I gave a squeal of delight and ran back with my find. Me, watchfinder and hero! My father thanked me and gave me a cuddle but was, this only struck me later, cooler than the occasion warranted. I thought about the matter for years until eventually I hit on the answer. My father hadn't believed me! Certainly it was unlikely that someone would find a watch in all those acres of sand. I realised my father must have put two and two together and come up with an explanation that seemed to make four. He had been for a swim and had presumably hidden the watch underneath his things. Then, I suppose he concluded, I must have crept up and taken the watch so I could have my great scene as watchfinder and hero. He thought I was a fraud, at least I thought he thought that. And I did turn into a fraud. Could I go up to him and say, Listen Dad, that business with the watch when we were by the seaside in the caravan, it wasn't the way you think it was, that I stole it, I mean . . . and he would have said, You think I think you stole it? What on earth put that idea into your head? Then I'd say, That's okay then, and it would have made everything even worse. Later on, when I was sixteen, seventeen, I used to get so furious with him. There were other things, not just the watch, things that happened when I should have been the great hero and ended up looking like a charlatan . . .'

Cora had heard the story before. If her professional reputation could have survived a third suicide among her patients she would have strongly recommended it to Mulders as a way out of his suffering.

'You look as if you're miles away.'

'Me? No. Go on with your story.'

Cora's current favourite fantasy was a role-swap. Nagy, in a white doctor's coat, would throw her without ceremony down onto the desk and, with brutal, proprietorial detachment, tear the clothes from her body (for this scenario she chose one of her older, shabbier dresses; ecstasy doesn't preclude one from being sensible), push her thighs so wide apart with his powerful arms that her hips shrieked with pain and ram an in every respect animal member (hairy, perhaps even covered in fleece!) into every possible bodily orifice.

What did Nagy so dislike about her consulting room? Van Gogh's *Sunflowers*? Perhaps he wanted to transfer their sessions to neutral ground in order to turn them into private conversations, i.e. not have to pay for them? Okay then. Perhaps she should have mentioned the possibility of free treatment explicitly. It was only the thought that the Devil would surely have been insulted by such an offer that had stopped her.

Mulders, the last guest on that day's chat show, finally left.

Cora called Tammie into the consulting room and asked her what she thought of the ambience. Imagine she were a patient coming here for the first time and seeing the desk and couch, the rolled-up yoga mat beside the cupboard. Was there something severe, offputting about the room? Tamara, having no idea what answer was expected of her, got out of it by saying she was so familiar with the room she couldn't see it objectively.

When she thought about how Nagy could have seen the only copy of the transcript of their session the obvious suspicion was that he had somehow got access to her filing cabinet. But how? Had he broken in during the night? Bribed the cleaning woman? Or Tammie? She was clutching at straws.

'Did Nagy ring?'

'No.'

'Did *you* give him my address?'

Cora didn't mean the question seriously. She could rely on Tammie. But the way she now looked at her boss, eyes wide open in an exaggerated show of obviously feigned surprise reminded Cora of Robert's cliché of there being a *rational* explanation for everything

'Out with it.'

'I didn't. Why should I?' The denial contained an element of uncertainty which gave Cora pause for thought. In average individuals of modest IQ such as Tammie the gestural and expressive symptoms of a lie were easy to identify, even without psychiatric training. Could it be true? Tammie, twenty-two, a blond pony-tail but otherwise generally mousy . . . ?

'Just tell me the truth.'

It was still a game, but this time Cora spoke in the tone of someone who already knew. Tammie, somewhat chubby, with little dress sense, began to stammer. She would never . . . No . . .

The strain was too much. Moisture began to collect in the corners of Tammie's eyes. She lacked the chutzpah to feign outrage at an unjust accusation. Easy meat for Cora, for whom the game was becoming horribly serious.

'He told me everything.'

'No!'

'How do you know?'

'But I don't know.'

'He thinks he's the Devil. What will promises mean to him? Even you might have thought of that?'

Tammie was incredibly stupid. Passed up her last chance to deny everything. Silence descended on the consulting room. Cora concealed the fact that she was trembling by wedging herself in the depths of her executive chair. Tammie as the rational explanation. Incredible.

'We just went out for a meal . . .'

'Abkhazian?'

The question broke Tammie's last resistance. She blubbered. Pathetic and revolting at the same time. Cora waved her to a chair. She had finally realised what Nagy found so awful about her practice. The girl he had squeezed his information out of then cast away like an empty orange skin.

'He ditched you?' At the end of the sentence Cora's voice

93

rose no more than a quarter-note. Any question spoken like that sounded like a statement of fact.

Tammie nodded. Punch-drunk.

'Do you know what you have done?'

Tammie stared at the floor, so defenceless it tore your heart strings. She was probably even happy that everything had come out.

'You've been sleeping with a patient.'

'No. Not that.'

'He didn't want to?'

Tammie gave a loud sob.

'YOU GAVE HIM INFORMATION! ABOUT ME! TO A LUNATIC!'

Cora didn't have to restrain herself any longer, had every right to be furious.

'I didn't know . . .'

'WHAT? WHAT DIDN'T YOU KNOW?'

The girl looked as if she was about to die of shame. Nagy had spoken to her weeks ago in Pullam's, asked to check her bag. Afterwards he had apologised and been so nice about it they had got talking, over a drink, on the house, on the ninth floor.

'That was before he came here. And he had only asked about you incidentally, in a general kind of way. How was my boss, did she treat me well, what kind of a reputation did she have . . . I didn't think anything of it.'

Of course. It went without saying.

Nagy had finished with Tamara. Did that mean he had also finished with the treatment? No. Otherwise he wouldn't have written that letter. Tammie had been sucked dry. Surplus baggage.

'I ought really to give you the sack, you realise that, don't you? Good. Now I want to hear everything. The whole bloody story from your lips. EVERYTHING!'

Tammie, all snot, sweat and tears, shot her a hopeful glance.

There wasn't much to tell. They'd just kissed, a bit of petting, in the park, after the restaurant. Cora's eyes narrowed. Nagy had stuck his tongue in there?!

'When he came to us, he asked me not to say anything . . .'

'But it was your *duty* to tell me.'

'I know that, but . . . I didn't know . . . and when I was typing the transcript, I mean, I had no idea he was on that kind of trip and I asked him about it because he never said anything about Maria Callas to me . . .'

'You gave him the transcript?'

'No. I just read it out to him. Not all of it. Just a little bit.'

'Precisely what bits?'

'Just your footnotes.'

'Aha.' Cora's lips parted.

'Yes. And then I asked him what's all this about? Are you serious about it?'

'And that was when he chucked you up?'

'No.'

'Aha!' Cora shot out of her chair and began pacing round Tammie in wide circles, her hands clasped behind her back.

'You didn't warn me, even though you would have good reason to suppose the fellow had some kind of designs on me?'

Tammie nodded.

'You know where he lives?'

Tammie nodded.

'You've been there?'

A nod.

'And slept with him?'

A shake of the head.

'He didn't put on any music for you?'

A shake of the head.

'What did you do then?'

A shake of the head.

'I ASKED WHAT YOU DID!'

'Just talked. Drank beer. I told him about my work, about the crazy types we get here.'

'And about me?'

'About you too.'

'Aha.'

Once she had gone to a bar with Nagy, a bar not far from his apartment, he probably often went there, the barman called him 'Stani'. Cora made her write down the name of the bar. And that was about everything Tammie, all sniffles and sobs, had to tell.

I'm one up on Nagy now. He won't have reckoned with Tammie's stupidity. At least not in the short term. He'll think he still has the advantage over me. Sweeping this rubber duck with a remote resemblance to a woman off her feet can't have given him much pleasure. He must have been desperately keen to get information about me. That's the way it must have been. Flattering, really.

That just leaves one question: what's he after?

Cora sat down, a black look on her face, her lips tight.

'You've been going round with a patient. Put me in danger. It's no good, we can't work together any longer.'

Tammie went white. 'But just now you said, if I told you everything . . .'

'Yes, I did say that.' Cora sighed and shrugged her shoulders, adopting a cold, pointed tone. 'But it's not possible. Just not possible. I'm *very* disappointed.'

Steel-clad silence.

The girl wouldn't cause any more difficulties, wouldn't talk to anyone who might possibly be a patient at some time in the future. Why send her away? I might even perhaps be able to make use of her.

I'll ring up tomorrow morning, grant her absolution, tell her she's graciously restored to favour.

For the moment, though, Cora was implacable, and strode to the lift without bothering to wipe up the soggy mess behind her.

Fiendish phone calls

Berlin: The police have issued warnings about an anonymous caller who talks to children on the phone and encourages

96

them to do things that will put their lives in danger. He told a ten-year-old boy in Berlin-Charlottenburg to place a bucket of water beside the telephone, plug in an electric appliance and put it in the water, holding it with both hands. When the boy objected he was afraid of an electric shock, the caller said it was an order from his father. Fortunately his fiendish attempt was unsuccessful. The boy hung up after the caller had made three wrong guesses at his father's Christian name.

15

La Lollo Rossa Bar, hidden away in the rear courtyard of a run-down tenement, seemed hardly to feel the need to advertise its existence. Its tiny neon-sign had a loose contact. It would flicker on for a few seconds, then go dark for minutes. Beside the steel-reinforced door stood a bottle bank and every step in the vicinity produced a crunch of glass. Cora, soaked by the drizzle, stood in the entrance of the building.

What am I doing going in there? I'll just make myself look ridiculous.

She had spent three hours wandering round, had eaten at the Sorrentino and was still asking herself the same question. When the waiter was making up the bill and asked which soup she had had, she could only remember the colour.

I have the initiative. What am I going to do with it?

Nagy had not been at home. Both windows of the bar had blinds. My turning up in the Lollo Rossa would certainly take the wind out of his sails, if he should happen to be in there. It would be a new situation, different, everything would be possible, everything.

Cora lit a cigarette, stared at the glowing tip, got smoke in her eyes.

The bar was a hundred yards from Nagy's flat. I went to see him, and when he wasn't in I tried a few bars in the neighbourhood. It was a possible line to take, but it didn't sound entirely convincing.

I'll have to be careful. This man has gone to a great deal of trouble. Because he's bored? He's got a gun in his pocket, and inside he's got the potential for aggression. What's going on in his head? What's going on in mine, for that matter, wanting to go in there? Curiosity × 9 = 1 dead cat.

Cora threw her cigarette away and plodded round the reinforced concrete and steamed-up windows of the tenement for the third time. It even occurred to her that Nagy could have deliberately laid the trail. Every step she took along it could be one step nearer his trap.

Rubbish! What am I doing? Exactly what my self-appointed Satan would want. I'm doing him the favour of demonising him.

Her feet hurt. Cora took the unsatisfying decision to look for a taxi to get her home. I'm making myself look ridiculous. How often had she already said that this evening? Dozens of times, and still she was hanging around here, in the rain, on broken glass, outside a dubious bar, where Nagy might well only go every couple of weeks, if at all. She remembered Robert asking whether she might not be getting just a tad overinvolved in the case of this Callas-freak? I should never have mentioned it. And then my reply! It's a psychologically fascinating phenomenon that requires fieldwork. Go home, you stupid cow!

Cora crossed the street and the courtyard and heaved her shoulder against the door of the bar. A wave of stale air and juke-box music washed over her. The plush seats and the red-and-pink colour scheme made the dive easy to classify without the help of various faces that screamed 'Previous convictions!' at you and the patent-leather basque the bar-woman was wearing. Two rooms. The one at the back was smaller and almost empty. An old Indiana-Jones pinball machine modified Cora's first impression. Not a clipjoint but a very downmarket juke-joint. Outwardly confident, but with knees trembling, she strode over to the table in the farthest corner.

'This is where you spend your free time? Isn't it a bit hackneyed for a devil?'

Nagy looked up from his beer, astonishment written all over his face.

'What makes you assume this is my free time?

The kind of answer that had made Cora fall in love with him.

'I was a bit worried about you.'

'Did I have an appointment?'

'Not an appointment . . .' She faltered and could find no good reason for her being here.

Nagy gestured towards a chair. 'Do sit down. I suppose Tamara's blown the gaff?'

Cora's response was not quite that of someone in control of the situation. '*Who!?*'

'It's quite natural I should make enquiries about you. Surely you didn't assume I would take just any old shrink into my confidence?'

Caught off her guard, Cora watched as the initiative scurried across the table into Nagy's welcoming arms.

'D'you like it here? It's quite nice once you get used to it. Are you thirsty? I'd buy you a half-bottle of champagne, or two even, only . . .'

'I know. You're temporarily embarrassed and there'd be the devil to pay if you asked for credit here.'

'How well you know me, madam. It's as if you could read my mind.'

Cora ordered two halves of the house *sekt* from the waitress, who scrutinised her suspiciously. When, on their arrival, immediate settlement of the bill was demanded and Cora indignantly rummaged round in her handbag for cash, Nagy discreetly directed his gaze at the floor.

'Just at the moment I am, unfortunately, in a situation which makes it impossible for me to do everything a perfect gentleman should.' He muttered the words, without looking up. Cora felt an urge to pat him, on the shoulder, on the cheek, to tell him it didn't matter. Nagy started and drew back when her hand moved across the table.

'Please . . .'

'What is it?'

'Let's drink to my health.'

At the bar were two blondes with small collared lizards in their hair which hissed venomously at each other while the blondes apathetically sucked their straws. The jukebox played through its entire repertoire, from A1 to K16. Mostly songs you could shuffle around on the dance-floor to. On a tiny stage framed by reflecting mirrors there was supposed to be a striptease act on the hour, every hour after ten o'clock. Anyone who asked what had happened to it was informed the girl was off ill.

'Actually, it's good that we met.' Nagy's voice sounded lethargic, almost sleepy.

'Why?'

The way he sipped at his champagne flute and kept the wine on his tongue for a long time – this was someone who either was in melancholy mood or had already drunk to his own health quite often that evening.

'You haven't had the end yet. The sad finale to my story.'

Once Nagy was in his role she would just be an anonymous audience and that was something Cora wasn't going to allow to happen.

'It's been pretty sad enough so far, apart from the bits where you were making fun of me.'

'When did I make fun of you?'

'Frequently.'

'Give me an example.'

'For example . . .' She pretended she was thinking.

'For example, anyone who is reasonably culturally aware knows there is no Callas recording of *Valkyrie*, but you play any old tape to me because you think I won't notice the difference.'

'Oh but there *is* a recording. *I* made it. I have many recordings I made myself direct from stage performances.'

Cora groaned, slapping herself on the side of the neck with both hands.

Sometimes I feel like I don't have a partner . . . The juke-box was playing 'Under the Bridge' by the Red Hot Chilli Peppers.

'These recordings you made . . .'

'Hm?'

'They must be worth quite a bit?'

'So? Oh, I see what you mean!' Nagy wrinkled his nose in distaste. 'Assuming your husband died and left you some very

101

personal memento, a lock of his hair, for example, would you sell it just because someone offered you money for it?'

Cora managed to pull back her spontaneous 'Yes' a fraction of an inch before it reached the tip of her tongue. *He's trying to worm out information about my marriage!*

'No.'

'There you are.'

In Cora admiration vied with her self-respect. She enjoyed being rhetorically shafted by Nagy. Only not so easily. And so quickly.

'Dammit, are you the least bit interested in whether I believe you or not? Or do you want me to restrict myself to just sitting back and listening?'

'Restrict yourself as much as you like. I should think you have limitless capacity in that direction.'

Nagy's tone of voice had immediately responded to her attack. His eyes were gleaming. Those unbelievably violet eyes.

'Why the nasty sting in the tail?'

'The butterfly asked the scorpion. Who replied . . .'

'What?'

'Exactly.' He gave a smug grin.

Cora felt she had made rather a mess of the discussion and didn't know whether to continue it, nor how. The room, with its stale tobacco smoke, seemed to be expanding, the walls to be moving apart. She took a sip from her glass. He took a sip from his. Didn't clink glasses. *He wants to get rid of me. He wants me to go. If he didn't, he'd say something within the next three seconds at the latest. Two. Three.*

'You'd buy another round, wouldn't you?'

'If my arm was twisted.'

'But I don't want you paying for me all the time.'

'What do you suggest?'

'In my flat there's a bottle of sixteen-year-old Lagavulin. Do you fancy a night-cap?'

As they left the bar Cora had the impression the barwoman gave Nagy an appreciative glance. *No problems this evening.*

I'm just imagining it. I should know that, if anyone. Obsessive over-interpretation of minor details had been the subject of her PhD viva.

Neither said a word during the short walk to his flat. The rain had stopped and the lift still stank of urine. Did no one here object? Telephone numbers, penises and matchstick women had been scratched on the paintwork of the lift door. Nagy, a head taller than Cora, clasped his hands at crotch level and stared sideways up at the ceiling. Cora suddenly realised how easy it must be for someone who lived in such a depressing environment to become addicted to an alternative reality. She was ashamed of getting angry at Nagy and remembered that her task was to heal patients, not to fight them.

Perhaps I only chose this profession in order to surround myself with sick people as a way of acquiring a bogus sense of superiority.

Nagy waved her to the greasy leather armchair and fetched the whisky from the balcony. The mound of wax looked horrible when there were no flames burning in it, the deformed, torched remains of some animal life, congealed, veinous, like the blobby mass you see in science fiction films when beaming-up malfunctions. Nagy gave his lips a thorough gnawing, swallowed them and looked round as if in search of something.

'I'm afraid I only own one glass.'

'Well at least there's some ice.' Cora pointed to the freezer.

'Unfortunately no. There's no ice in it. Just a moment, there must be another glass in the cellar. Yes. Excuse me a minute. Make yourself at home.'

He urged her into the chair and went out into the corridor.

Cora would have dearly loved to have a look in the freezer, but the melted wax formed a seal that was 100% tamperproof. She had a rummage through the records and tapes, but found nothing of interest.

The dressing table beside the bed. Two drawers.

You'll have to be quick about it.

The top drawer contained pornographic magazines. Nothing kinky or specialised for fetishists; nothing you wouldn't find on your local supermarket shelf. Tasteful, high-gloss sex for the average fantasy.

Cora felt a mixture of relief and larcenous pleasure, just as she had when, as a teenager, she emerged from a store with a pair of tights under her vest. She listened. Uncertain how much time she had left, she put the magazines back, straightened out the pile then opened the other drawer. Standing on the bottom, arms raised, was a doll. A girl in a petticoat, with white stockings, the height of a pencil. It said something in a squeaky voice. Cora quickly shut the drawer; heard something fall over onto the wooden drawer bottom.

Nonsense. Not a voice. A squeaking hinge.

'You're not getting bored?' Nagy sounded uneasy.

'No . . .' Cora stared at the ceiling, even though there wasn't much of interest to see there. Her knees and elbows were trembling. She had managed to throw herself back into the chair at the last moment.

A touch of the button and music with Italian words came, words such as 'pietà' and 'traditor' suggesting a heroic plot. The single malt had a delicious aroma.

Was it too stuffy in the room, he enquired, too warm? She looked rather hot.

Nagy was sitting cross-legged on the bed, his head swaying from side to side to the long, sweeping melodies. Holding up his whisky glass like a magic crystal ball on the palm of his right hand, he jerked his chin towards the stereo system in a wordless toast. The rims of their glasses touched.

'It's 'A Masked Ball',' he said.

'Life?'

'The tape. Verdi. 'Un ballo in maschera'. Milan '57.'

She assumed she was supposed to say something. She raised her eyebrows.

'That was the year she started to go downhill. The long decline of the goddess. At a glamorous ball in Venice. No one had the least suspicion, apart from me. The glass you have in your hand is a souvenir of that evening. Maria drank out of it the first time she drank to Onassis. Why are you grimacing like that?'

'Oh . . . no, that's . . . great! As if you were drinking out of the bowl Socrates had his hemlock in. Have you got that as well?'

'Not any more. My cellar's small. I had to part with a lot of things.' At least now a trace of playfulness had appeared in his voice. When she asked whether the glass was perhaps connected with unpleasant memories his answer was a sad smile.

'It was my own choice. No trick was too mean. Sometimes, if Toy's teeth hadn't been so harmless I could have bitten Maria, so strong was my hatred of her. Then I went through phases when I felt sorry for her, when having to watch her decline cut my heart to tiny ribbons. The fact that these phases gradually began to dominate is connected with my increasing softness. The rules of the game had changed. Once her beauty was gone for good, once the doll had been broken, the game itself had lost its point. It had become too obvious, too easy, boring, played out. No new tricks for two old dogs.

'Are we playing a game too?'

'The two of us? Hmm . . . No . . . no, not like playing a game of chess. Like playing a shellac record perhaps.'

Nagy downed the generous measure in his second glass. It soon started to affect his speech. He swallowed some syllables while drawing out others interminably.

Satan, in his cups, explaining the world to some satyrs. Isn't there an old picture with that title? If there isn't someone ought to forge one into existence.

'During her marriage to Meneghini Toy was very important. Maria showered more tenderness on the poodle than on anyone else. Which I used to my advantage. There were years when I spent so much time inside that dog that I got out of practice walking on two feet. Toy was allowed to sit on Maria's lap when she flew in an aeroplane. He never had to travel in the hold. If, despite his knitted pullover, he caught a cold, she summoned the best doctors. You can't imagine the fuss that was made over that beast. There were crooks who planned to kidnap Toy and demand a ransom. Not a bad idea. What crime is so cost-effective? If you're caught you get away with a fine! Once one of those gangs even managed to get into Maria's hotel room. They were just about to grab the pooch, when I emerged from its ears. You should have seen the looks on their faces. Did they run!' Nagy snorted with laughter. 'At last there's someone I can tell the story to.'

He wasn't squatting any more, he had taken his shoes off and was lying down on the bed. Eyes closed, humming happily to himself, he found the most comfortable position, placed his whisky glass on his chest and clasped his hands behind his head:

'Gradually everything changed. Toy became less important to her.

Onassis stole into Maria's life. Slowly, cunningly, he led her into a world where the faithful Meneghini looked even duller than he really was, a world where he simply withered away like an organ cut off from its blood supply. There was no escape for Maria. Fear was always at her shoulder, whispering, You mustn't spare yourself. She was on fire. Surrounded by the fat of the social body, parasites who basked in the reflected glow of her glory and at the same time gave themselves airs, Maria never developed a sense for who played an important role, who was merely one of the extras. A parvenu herself, she was always afraid she might wake to find the dream had gone, that kitschy dream of yachts, receptions, exiled princes, gala evenings, casinos, palm-fringed beaches, the whole fifties Côte d'Azur and jet-set nonsense. You should have seen Maria's apartment in Verona! A nightmare of imitation rococo! Floral wallpaper, a pink bathroom full of gold mirrors, a bedroom full of silver- and gold-plated swans! Even Mad King Ludwig and Jeff Koons collaborating under the influence of LSD couldn't have come up with something like that. No sirree!'

He filled his glass a third time.

'As a parvenu Onassis was fully her equal. His millions had been made in one generation, *his*. He was Maria's counterpart, only in the masculine variant. Greed instead of longing. He, the richest man in the world, lusted after the most famous woman in the world. Sounds somehow logical, doesn't it?

Makes sense. At least it would in a primer on breeding pedigree animals. I admired Onassis as a colleague. Oh yes, he was a fiend. From my lips that's a compliment. His yacht, the *Christina* –' Nagy's voice sank to a whisper. 'There were forty-two telephones, sixty staff and one genuine El Greco. The bar stools were covered in whale foreskin. Need I say more . . . Oh, and he couldn't stand opera.'

At first Cora thought she was seeing things. Two tears were running down Nagy's cheeks. He wiped them away, furtively, disguising it by rubbing his temples, cheeks, neck and shoulders with both hands. The glass on his chest jiggled and swayed.

'Maria would put up with very little, except from Onassis. She could be violent, could scream, spit, kick. Sometimes she threw inkwells. 'The Tigress', that was her other nickname, when she wasn't being 'La Divina'. Then the photo was published.'

'The photo?'

'Yes. An icon needs ornaments. Lots of them. Anecdotes, rumours. Climbing plants that need something to entwine themselves round if they are to exist at all. After that picture appeared anything was possible, any rumour, any invention, any slander, nothing was too improbable. Here –' He felt under the bed and threw something into Cora's lap.

'It happened in Dallas. A bailiff nailed her in her dressing room, immediately after the performance, and handed her a payment order her former agent had obtained against her. She poured a torrent of foul abuse over the innocent bearer. A news photographer got the picture of his life. The picture that transformed Maria into a foul-mouthed Fury. I placed him there, I aimed his camera. No trick was too dirty for me. The next moment I was ashamed of myself, my name, my nature, I was the humble dog desperate to make up for what it had done. That photo was the root of her legend. Priceless. Have you seen the stupid look on the bailiff's face? And that Maria is still in costume as Butterfly. I was proud of that picture. I was promoting her legend by fair means or foul, I wanted something that went beyond the banal. Simultaneously I found it repugnant – for the very first time! – that in order to achieve that I had to subject a living human being to such torment. I had never had any scruples before, never! Now I was caught between different sides of my nature and saw myself alternately as a swine and a benefactor. I was both, of course, and happy with neither. And as if that wasn't enough evil . . . Oh –'

'Don't you feel well?'

'No. I even exploited her mother, whom I had forgotten to dispose of. Evangelia would so dearly have loved to share in her daughter's fame. She kept on writing begging letters, suing for royalties, so to speak. It was her upbringing alone, she claimed, that had led to Maria becoming world famous. Then one day Maria replied. And what a reply! I still have the letter.' Nagy was suddenly holding a yellowed, tattered sheet of paper in his hand; he must have taken it out from under his pillow. He read it aloud, making his voice higher and managing to sound convincingly female. Uncanny.

'Don't come to me with your difficulties. I've had to work for my money and you're young enough to work as well. And if you can't earn your living you can always jump out of the window or drown yourself.'

Nagy grinned, but his lips seemed to lose their strength and sagged into a sad droop.

'Not a very nice letter, eh? I dressed up as one of the paperazzi and persuaded Evangelia to hand it over. It was immediately translated into a hundred languages for the gossip columns of the whole world. Oh, hell . . .'

'Would you have liked to have written something like that to *your* mother?'

'Nice try . . . The great thing about Maria was that she stuck to her guns. Nowadays any minor celebrity would immediately make it up with mummy in front of a battery of cameras, claiming it was only a joke, a private code, a distorted translation, whatever. Maria did nothing of the kind. Never saw her mother again. NEVER again. Heheh . . . To keep the wolf from the door Evangelia had to sell dolls she made herself. Dolls representing Maria's most popular roles, Norma,

Traviata, Lucia, Tosca. I'm not one to boast, but can you imagine a more fiendish torture? Sometimes I got back into top form again. It's a long time ago now. Maria went through hell. She thought that in the eyes of the world her reputation always depended on her next performance. Every evening she was appearing not on stage, but before a court that was sitting in judgment on her. And every ovation was only a conditional discharge. There were always photographers buzzing round her like insects on a sultry day. She enjoyed it, until fear struck. When she missed her first high notes, or, even more so, when she had a triumph which seemed unsurpassable, making her think the peak of her career would soon be behind her.

There are reports of ski jumpers who, in spite of all their experience, are physically sick before every jump. Something like that was true of Maria. The little band of enemies was always there, waiting for the slightest slip; immediately the whistling, hissing, booing would start. You have a kind of person here on earth who can only tolerate greatness and beauty when it's dead, if at all, people who get a self-righteous pleasure out of tearing the best to pieces. Maria's fears grew to pathological proportions. It's easy to say it's your own fault, why do you make things so difficult for yourself? Can't you cheat a little, take dangerous notes down an octave or slide over them? But that's not the way legends are created. Maria always went for it, was always on a knife-edge, triumph or disaster. And whichever it was, both merely served to increase her fears.'

He thrust out his lower lip and let his head drop. Then he looked round, as if he had just woken up, and took a deep breath, mouth wide open.

'I need to get out. Let's go for a walk, shall we? I'm sorry, but this room's unbearable.'

Cora had no objections. She would have preferred it if Nagy had stayed lying on the bed, getting drunk, and had raped her there rather than elsewhere, but if rape wasn't on the agenda, then it didn't matter.

He offered her his coat, but she refused. It had stopped raining. The temperature outside was still a good fifty degrees.

They headed west where, three streets further on, the red-light district began. The sex shops and souvenir kiosks stayed open until well past midnight. This was the tourist part where the police kept an eye on things. In the chestnuts along the canal bank were strings of coloured bulbs and spotlights, giving the water a reddish shimmer. The effect was very picturesque. Old couples, coach parties, even school classes walked along past the tarts. Advertising holograms for the blue-movie cinemas flooded the streets with colour. Drug dealers announced themselves to passers-by with a Psst! The slightest response and they trotted out their list of wares. *Dope, speed, coke?* Nagy had the Lagavulin in his coat pocket. Cora was embarrassed when he handed her the bottle and men in tartan caps shouted 'Cheers!' or 'Wheyhey!' He clicked his fingers, as he had done in the store, and a yellow rosebud appeared in his hand. He didn't give it to Cora, but, click! the rose was in the water.

'Maria's views on marriage were very conservative. She had no idea about sex. Adultery was a mortal sin for her. When Roberto Rossellini and Ingrid Bergman separated she crossed them both off her list of friends. Just imagine when a woman like that finally sees the light. Wham! bam! her whole world is overturned in one single night. She got a divorce and her relationship with Onassis was made public. For a few months he loved her, preening himself on his trophy. Then his cock started looking for new worlds to conquer. I can't even say I blame him for it. But the fact that he lied to Maria for years, promising to marry her and managing to put her off until everything was ready for the conquest of Jackie Kennedy, *that* made me furious. Maria's voice, on which she made great demands as it was, suffered from the strain, began to wear out. Long before her time. At an age when other singers are only just approaching the peak of their career.'

Nagy's drunkenness had now reached the stage where it was obvious to the eye in the way it affected his gait and gestures. He had emptied the bottle almost unaided and slung it at a wastepaper basket. It missed.

'Onassis, he wanted to buy up the whole world, oh, the way

he treated Maria once he had her in his thrall! The way he humiliated her! "Who do you think you are?" he would scream at her. "You're nothing. A nobody with a worn-out pipe in your throat." To say I had mixed feelings when I heard him say that is putting it mildly. I was the divided beast that never knew whether to laugh or cry, to mourn or rejoice.'

'If you hated Onassis . . . ?'

'Hmmm?'

'Why didn't you . . . ? I mean . . . ?'

'Punish him?'

'Yes.'

'But he was necessary! For the legend. And even if I did sometimes feel like doing it, Maria loved him. That neutralised my power.'

'Like garlic with vampires?'

'I don't know any vampires. Do you?'

'Only from the cinema.'

'You can keep your stupid cinema. This wasn't a film. It was . . . it . . . WAS! Still is! I won't let you make fun of it.'

'Sorry.'

'Maria was burning out before my very eyes! A goddess, flogging herself to death, turning to ashes. She herself thought it was a temporary weakness. She fought against it, dogged as ever, only this time all the exertion of her will-power was in vain. Tutta finita sulla terra . . . that was the time when the white poodle left us. Left the future to me like a pile of rubbish. Didn't say goodbye to anyone.'

'Where are we heading for anyway?'

Nagy seemed to have some route in mind and was striding purposefully through the maze of streets and alleyways. Not a stroll any more. Cora had difficulty keeping up with him and was getting out of breath. When she pointed out how quickly he was walking he scarcely showed any reaction.

'Why do some cats climb up trees from which they can't get down? And why do others jump out of the third or fourth floor onto asphalt? Some want to be free to roam. Others prefer to be saved by the fire brigade'

'What is it you're trying to say?'

111

'There are cats and cats.'

'Anything else?'

'Some disguise themselves as poodles, others as psychiatrists.'

'For a sick man you can be bloody supercilious!'

'I will assume a more modest mien.'

They must be close to the docks, in the seamy part of the red-light district. Sailors' dives with girls' names, often only the size of a sitting room, became frequent. Drunken marines in groups of four or five blocked Cora's way, greeted her with heavy-breathing familiarity, invited her to have a drink with them, surrounded her, making suggestive compliments. Nagy did nothing about it. Pretended he wasn't with her. Even seemed to find it funny.

A military police patrol came round the corner and the marines trotted off, meek as little lambs. Cora was destined not to find out whether the situation could have become awkward or not.

'What's all this about. What are we doing here?'

Nagy's chin dropped to his chest and bounced back up, as if his breastbone was a trampoline. His eyelids flicked up and down in time.

'Madama, I'm pissed.'

'A statement of the obvious.'

'For a good reason. A very good reason. Guess.'

'You're desperate, a sick man.'

'Assertions of which the third is the most insulting. And yet, soon you won't be all that wrong . . .' He made an uncoordinated gesture, the meaning of which was impossible to decipher.

'It was more fun when the white poodle was here. At the time I thought that when he went he would leave the field to me and that would be great. But without an opponent the game's not worth the candle. What's the point? I have, Madama, reached a momentous decision. I have decided –' he took a deep breath, 'to commit suicide.'

'No you won't.'

'Oh yes I will!' He snorted. 'I have an ulterior motive. To be dead. Eventually.'

'Cunning.'

'Isn't it? Dead and with Maria.' Nagy tried to shake the alcohol out of his head, supporting himself against the wall of a building. 'The way of dying I've chosen is a lengthy one. Would you like to know which?'

'Hmm?'

'I will become human and then I'll die in the way chance happens to have reserved for me. Isn't that what you want, Signora?'

'How are you going to do it? "Become human", is it that simple?'

'On the contrary, it's extremely tedious. Probably. I've no idea, really. But I'm attracted by the idea of being an old man sitting with other old men and saying, "Lads, I used to be the devil himself!" And they'll all have a laugh or a grin and only I'll know what really was. That and a beautiful sunset. I'm sure that would make me happy . . . outrageously happy . . .'

'That's what you see as your future? Just dying?'

'Why ever not?' Nagy's speech was interspersed with hiccoughs. 'I'm completely fed up with everything. Why do I keep hanging on here? What for? Who for? Having to make do with a few kids who celebrate weird masses in my name? Eh? Should I play the call boy with the ice-cold jism', his voice grew loud, 'FOR A FEW FRIGID CATHOLIC CUNTS WHO GO SCREWY 'CAUSE THEY DON'T GET SCREWED?'

'Shh! You're drunk.'

'Yes. Oh dear. What's it like being human? Hmm? I'm a bit afraid of it. There are some dreadful examples that really put you off. Cora? May I call you Cora? Let's call each other Cora . . . I probably wouldn't be a very good person, would I?'

Nagy gave a crazy laugh, staggered. Cora grabbed his arm and supported him. She could smell the alcohol on his breath.

'Don't touch!'

Cora let go. Nagy's fingertips touched the pavement.

'You're ruining my patina. It's taken me centuries to get it right.'

'Your self-pity is insufferable.'

113

'Self-pity?' Nagy pulled himself together, stamping on the pavement, as if to prove he could walk straight. Fast-moving clouds were swirling round the moon.

'Self-pity, eh?'

'I'm here to help you.'

'Of course . . .'

He came up to her until he was only inches away, put his hands on the wall over Cora's head and whispered something that sent her wild. 'Pull up your skirt.'

She did what he demanded without thinking. There were many things going on inside her head, but the desire to have Nagy grope her dominated everything.

He clicked his fingers.

'Okay.'

'What?'

'Just interested. To see how far gone you were . . .'

With that he disappeared round the corner, she could hear the clatter of his footsteps on the cobbles. Cora's first thought was to dash after him, but instead she screamed, hissed and snorted with white-hot fury and set off running, for a few hundred yards, until it occurred to her that Nagy was probably just looking for a dark corner where he could spew up his guts unobserved. Of course. That was it.

He won't have abandoned me here? Here! He's not that type. Is he looking for me? Why doesn't he call out? Why doesn't he shout my name? Skeletal houses, empty of glass. Puddles with no light reflected in them. A wind-driven dampness. And sailors, sailors everywhere. Without moving, Cora slid deeper into the silence. Cowered in a garage entrance, freezing, until a chance taxi took pity.

Rome: The beach at Ostia was the scene of a bizarre crime. The body of 27-year-old Fabio C. was discovered with a gherkin stuck in his throat. He had choked to death. As the post-mortem showed, the victim had twice managed to bite off a portion of the murder weapon.

WEEK 4

16

WEDNESDAY, THURSDAY, FRIDAY

Robert didn't like it when his wife was ill. He wasn't the man for tender loving care, but he looked after her, did what was necessary and did it meticulously. The way you would take care of an orchid. He would have preferred it if he could have taken her illness upon himself and sweated it out in bed, alone, without making demands on anyone. It wouldn't have been an act of mercy, simply the lesser of two evils.

Aspirin, herbal infusions, magazines – the things he brought to her bedside were acknowledged, at best tolerated. Cora remained silent, and her expression seemed to say, whatever you bring, I don't need it; everything else, I do.

If he left her in peace, her silence when he went to see her again had an even more reproachful note: You haven't brought it.

Robert felt like protesting, So what? If it's a bit of excitement you want, there's plenty out there. Go and get it. No one will object. Just don't look at me as if I were your prison.

He said nothing. Lugged the television from the living room upstairs.

Cora knew that she *wanted* to be ill. Her skin wanted to be grey and brittle, her neck stiff; her temples wanted to be bells someone was striking with a pick-axe.

My life has all the élan of a rusty old musical box. The princess on the musical box, in her rightful place beside the pillow, is wallowing in nostalgia, whether she wants to or not; she makes her pirouettes, such fast pirouettes that no one notices the creaking that has accompanied them for some time now. Her yellowing tutu wrinkled all the way up to her forehead.

A married woman. A marriage of mutual inconvenience. When Cora looked back on her life it seemed to her like a stretch of water which, when it tried to put on airs merely ended up with a scum of bubbles on the surface.

She had rung up Tammie, forgiven her, as planned, and asked her to cancel all her chat shows for the rest of the week. And what had Tammie done? Handed in her notice, and with immediate effect! Because, she said, it would be impossible for them to re-establish a healthy working relationship; she would, she said, feel unhappy in the poisoned atmosphere. Also, could you believe the cheek!, because she objected to sessions being described as 'chat shows' and sick people as 'inadequates'. And having spoken, she put down the receiver without so much as a 'Thank you, ma'am.'

Cora's first reaction was not anger but envy. Envy of Tammie's newly acquired self-respect, her ability to act on a decision, to take on the risk of a new beginning. While she herself was lying in bed, flued up to the eyeballs and unable to get Nagy out of her mind.

Hatred came to join love. Unpeaceful coexistence. One didn't take over from the other, they were equally strong and just confronted each other, got on each other's nerves.

To become human. A nice idea, a necessary one, almost. Somehow or other he has to harmonise the process of ageing with his fantasy world. Find an explanation for annoying facts.

Cora took refuge in her favourite video, *Gone with the Wind*. Scarlett O'Hara holding a turnip before the backdrop of a dark-red sky.

'I'LL NEVER GO HUNGRY AGAIN!'

There was one way of stripping Nagy of his defences. That was to dig up his true biography somewhere or other and rub his nose in it. Shock therapy. Outcome uncertain. He might break down in relief. Or go raving mad, ripe for the padded cell.

I'LL NEVER LOOK RIDICULOUS AGAIN!

On Friday morning a letter arrived.

Dear Cora,
I do hope you agree to overlook the little contretemps my inebriation caused. Without the help of strong liquor, mutating into a coarse

*human being would be very tedious. And I was coarse, wasn't I?
Pretty good for a start, don't you think? Look on it as proof of a
successful therapy. Of course, there's still quite some time to go before
I'm an old man boasting to other old men. Pity you'll just see me in
my declining years. Without wanting to boast, I wish we'd met long
ago, when I was still in my pomp and majesty.*

How much more crap are you going to dump on me?

*I often think of Maria during the time when she was trying to get
back to being as perfect as she used to be; when she would step onto
the stage, trembling with fear, determined to give her all; and that all,
each desperate effort of will, produced nothing but a shadow of her
former glory. At first the applause was scarcely any less rapturous.
Maria's legend made up for a lot. In recordings, with the rests she
needed between takes, and especially in lower roles such as Carmen,
there were still glittering triumphs. But recordings could not satisfy her
soul. She needed the stage, her audience. Needed them and at the
same time went through agonies at each performance that was less
than perfect, at applause that was directed not at her, but at her
monument, at the stone colossus she bore in her body.*

*From inside a poodle you see things from a different perspective.
You're closer to the ground, to the dust, to sweaty feet. Get your nose
literally rubbed in the misery from which a legend is distilled. At times
I found it unbearable. I wanted to shout out — yap out — to potential
figures in the legend, Behave yourselves! Act in a dignified and tragic
manner, choose your words as if they were being recorded live. Human
beings can be so embarrassing, but I don't need to tell you that.*

Cora's fighting spirit awoke, stretched out in bed beside her
and asked, bleary-eyed, Are we going to put up with that?

*When Maria began to suspect that Onassis was going to leave her, she
invented a child. Pointed to her belly and demanded the contents be
made legitimate. Onassis bawled at her, threatening to leave her at
once unless she got rid of the brat. Partly because of his power over her,
and partly in order to mould the situation to her advantage, Maria
found a doctor whom she paid well to fake an abortion. An abortion*

with complications in a late stage of pregnancy. Huge loss of blood. Can one blame her? Unfortunately it was counterproductive. Onassis did not get a guilty conscience at all. On the contrary, he decided to make sure Maria's belly really had been emptied. The quack was fond of money and so the whole sorry farce came to light. Onassis had had enough. And somehow that was understandable too. Maria had herself carried to the yacht, all pale make-up, sacrifice and renunciation etched on her features, the embodiment of tragedy, only to be received with mocking laughter. Onassis and the expensive abortionist were leaning over the railing, clinking cognac glasses, shouting wheee-ooo!, giggling drunkenly and making gynaecological gestures. The scene used to be one of my favourites, a highlight of my collection; now I find it shallow and sad, too black even for the Devil.

In 1965, in Paris, the Tigress collapsed on stage, only a shadow of her former self, the one-time acrobat of the voice now just managing the mezzo range. With the help of injections she had made heroic efforts to struggle through the performance, but no longer had the strength to change costume before the third act. At the time I thought, That's enough, thought it would be right if she died there and then. Breathed her last like Verdi's Traviata. Didn't manage to pick herself up and go on with the pointless, hopeless struggle. To my regret, it continued for years. With her repeated, ever more awful comebacks, Maria was unconsciously fighting against her own legend. She sang her head off like a half-demented raven, but it made no difference. Her fame had long since set up alone and couldn't care less what she did. When a legend becomes too powerful, the living person gets in the way.

Sometimes, at moments when she was particularly depressed, she would have been capable of doing a deal, of signing a pact with anyone at all. But by that time it was too late. I can only bring out of a human being something that's there inside them. Apart from the cold embryo of the icon, there was nothing left inside Maria, she had given everything, chopped up everything in her attempt to keep the fire of her genius burning. And she hadn't even needed me to do it. However much I wanted to play a role in Maria's life, I never had more than a walk-on part. A minor source of irritation. You know the feeling? I think you do. Let's be honest: you'd like to play a role in my life, be something more than just the psychiatrist. You can understand what it feels like to come up against a brick wall, to be of no use whatsoever.

'No dogs.' *When I read that inside my poodle skin, I always wanted to whine. Did whine. Sometimes.*

As a psychiatrist you didn't try to impose yourself on me, and I'm grateful for that. As a woman you tried everything you could. Wasted effort, unfortunately, on an unsuitable object. You can't have everything, you don't need everything. My cellar is, as I said, very small.

You little Beelzebugger! You mean fucking arsehole!

You're probably swearing at me, even more probably you'll soon have forgotten me. I'm off now to buy the latest edition of The Watchtower. *In its pages the world still makes sense. I'm such a sentimental old Devil . . .*
Farewell,
S.

Let a fellow like that escape, untreated, unhealed? No, never!

She leapt out of bed, got dressed and dropped her illness in the dirty-linen basket.

'Where are you going? Are you better?'

The front door slammed shut.

Robert breathed a sigh of relief and picked up scissors and newspaper.

He had not always been this oasis of calm that his heart trouble compelled him to be. There had been affairs, overtime worked because of the affairs, quarrels because of the overtime. There had been times when Cora had accused him of being a workaholic, when they had sworn and shouted at each other. Making up afterwards had been equally passionate. Then came the operation and everything changed. Had to change, calm down. No more violent scenes. Anything that wasn't slow, leisurely, effortless, involved what the surgeon called an *orgasm of risk*. More than two *orgasms of risk* per month would have been negligent to the point of leaving his wife a widow. And he had no intention of doing that to her, or to himself.

121

Sonthofen, Bavaria: A young farmer from the Allgäu region spent months making an electric chair, even dismantling metal parts from electricity pylons for it. His mother came into the room one evening and switched on the light, setting off the electric charge that killed her son. The police called it a suicide that was unparalleled in its cruelty. The mother and son had lived alone together on the isolated farm for 20 years.

17

SATURDAY

Bursting with an energy that didn't know what to do with itself, Cora sat in a number 14 bus, got out after two stops and got on the bus going in the opposite direction. In this way she drove up to five times per hour past the tenement block where Nagy lived, sufficiently camouflaged by sunglasses, hat and grubby window.

Just to see him was an event. A surreptitious pleasure. Afterwards the air seemed light, gravity transformed into youth. Walking, her soles seemed to caress the street.

To engage a detective would have been too expensive. Perhaps not too expensive, but how could she have justified the expenditure to Robert. She should have got a secret account long ago. Or a new accountant.

Love and hate. Such unfamiliarly extreme emotions. Everything was new. Exciting and shattering. White and black, like white and black poodles. What's your mother's name?

Once, in the afternoon, she saw him out jogging. In tracksuit trousers and sweat-soaked T-shirt. She felt he was playing a part, mocking her with the ordinariness of it. He didn't look up at all, and turned off into the next side-street.

She had not taken Nagy's letter as a farewell. He was just playing hard to get.

The sky was grey from the ghosts of poisoned pigeons. Dr Dulz's practice is closed this week. Emergency cases should relieve themselves in complete confidence in the empty space after the pips. Bugproof and unending, thanks to automatic tape-change.

'So he has a gun. And? Has he ever used it?'

'No . . .'

'What makes you so sure it's real?'

'I don't know. I mean I'm not a hundred percent sure.'

'And you don't know whether Nagy is his real name either?'

'No.'

'Don't you require any identification from your patients?'

'Now wait a minute!'

'Okay, I'm waiting. What do you actually want?'

Lioba Rosenbaum had been at university with Cora and after graduation had specialised in criminal psychology. She had ended up working at one of the district police stations. Her ambition was to cross swords with hostage-takers, her daily bread looking after rape victims. She sounded less like an interested colleague, more like a harassed official. Reluctantly she entered *Nagy, Stanislaus* into the police computer. Without success.

'Now what? I'm telling you Cora, there's no point. You can report him for possession of firearms without a licence and we'll check him out. But this kind of unofficial enquiry . . .'

Cora explained once more. An extremely aggressive patient, highly suicidal by his own admission – 'Should I just leave him out there? Wait till he runs amok? He's been nosing about in my private affairs. He's a danger, to himself and to others. To get to him I need information . . .'

Lioba Rosenbaum shrugged her shoulders. It was hardly a criminal act to go to a doctor under a false name and then break off the treatment. And that he thinks he's the devil, well . . . Why not go for compulsory detention in a mental hospital?

'I don't think it would work.'

Patient N., an extremely talented actor with the devil's own gift of the gab, would deny everything, dismiss it as a joke. And enjoy himself into the bargain.

'It's not just his identity I'm interested in. He's a phoney, a charlatan. I'm sure you must have had him here before. I could bring you a fingerprint.'

'Cora, please . . .'

'It's his name. Don't you understand? It's like Rumpelstiltskin. Call the devil by his real name and you'll tear him apart.'

'Cora!'

'What?'

She'd gone and done it again.

Nagy, standing up in the boat and draped in black cloth, is being rowed to the Isle of the Dead, where Maria is waiting for him on the beach. In a shining white cocktail dress. At the edges of the picture Böcklin and Munch are still painting in the last specks of foam and don't realise they are already on air.

A yacht crosses the wake of the small boat, causing it to sway. The figure at the oars falls into the sea. Nagy does the rest of the journey on foot, starts running over the water and throws off the sweat-soaked cloth.

Her patient was haunting her dreams. To get her own back in the real world was legitimate self-defence.

Cora's actions were dictated by some obscure instinct, which went far beyond prestige and lust. It was as if Nagy represented a crossroads, a key to the direction her future life would take. An acid test she would pass or fail.

The boats for trips round the harbour were anchored along the promenade, every jetty bright with flags. A police motor launch glided noisily along past the quay. Clouds that had been conscripted into poetic service paraded lethargically across the sky. At the front of her mind Cora was trailing her fingers in the water, at the back of her mind a 'scorched-earth strategy' was forming. I could risk having him committed to an asylum for the criminally insane, but once in there, who would look after him? Not me.

For late September the evenings were unnaturally warm.

The prospect of spending future winters commuting between her practice and their terraced house. Between Robert and other sick persons. Shunted from one ritual to another, day in day out.

Softened light streams past, seeking refuge, a hundred years old, no older, arranged for cello and viola. Plaintive as a recorder. Shortly before sunset a Bach trumpet joins in. The deceiving hour of memory, of open questions and open wounds. When the winds come shuffling along like a funeral cortege and pass without a word of acknowledgment.

The forces of emergency power and darkness were in conference inside her head, shouting and swearing at each other. The only thing they were both agreed on was that the conference room was too cramped, too stuffy. Powerful emotions were busy with bone saws, trying to make room for themselves, open up space above the top of her skull. Stale air escaped, a pleasant feeling of emptiness spread. A no-man's-land between the fronts. A minefield for any attempt at interpretation. How beautiful it all was . . . wasn't it? The sea air and the smell of the heavy oil in the tankers.

There must be a last vestige of faintheartedness inside her. Somewhere between larynx and solar plexus there was still something pulling her back. Since she was pulling the other way, the result was a lively tug-of-war. Ambitious oriental girls, who had had an operation to change their almond eyes to the western model, marched determinedly along the canal.

The princess on the musical-box saw a very blunt object coming towards her and raised her slender arms, the way she always did. It was no use. The object, normally employed as a shoe, had no scruples and a princess's forehead meant no more to it than any other piece of plastic.

Mother had fossilised embryo in her womb for 60 years
Vienna: A minor medical sensation in Austria. A 92-year-old woman in Vienna had a fossilised embryo in her womb for 60 years.

Doctors Paul Speiser and Konrad Brezina only discovered it when they x-rayed the woman, who had been admitted to a hospital in Vienna with pneumonia.

The foetus had died in about the 31st week of pregnancy. After that, Dr. Speiser explained, a layer of calcium had been deposited round the embryo, more or less fossilising it. Their patient died two weeks after being admitted to the hospital.

Her son said that when she was 32 his mother had believed she was expecting her fourth child. She had suddenly suffered severe abdominal pains, but then recovered. According to experts, the fossilisation of the embryo occurs once in every 250,000 pregnancies. There was, however, only one other known case, which occurred in the 1930s in China.

WEEK 5

18

FRIDAY, SATURDAY

Dawn, grey with a mourning-band. Furred meadows.

Robert found the tomcats lying beside each other in the garden, dead. No external signs of violence. To take the corpses to the vet for an autopsy seemed unnecessary. What apart from poison could have brought both their lives to an end in the same night? What was irritating was the lack of any motive. When alive, the tomcats had not got on anyone's nerves, never wandered into foreign territory nor yowled with feline lust. Robert examined Fred and Frith's communal bowl, sniffed tuna-fish remains, scoured the lawn and pond for pieces of meat someone might have thrown over the hedge. Nothing.

At breakfast Cora's response was very composed. She immediately set about discussing the disposal of the corpses. The animal crematorium or the organic compost heap? A family grave in the garden or unauthorised disposal in the park?

Eventually she handed Robert the spade and pointed to a spot by the hedge. Whilst her husband, with an expression of revulsion on his face, was using the tip of his shoe to manoeuvre the cadavers in the direction indicated, Cora, without shedding a tear or saying a prayer over them, headed for work. His irritation at her behaviour was outweighed by his relief at the calmness with which she had accepted the demise of their entire stock of pets.

'Will you be back before the evening?'

'No.'

Perhaps it wasn't poison? Perhaps it was just old age, solidarity even unto death. Not to say a gay *Liebestod*. A neat interpretation can turn anything into an amusing anecdote. Things would be unbearable otherwise.

Robert rang the Nude Cleaning Service to see whether they had a female employee free later that morning. A blonde, if possible, who would not consider garden work beneath her.

A little risk now and then, in small doses, be the bold hero now and then . . .

Nagy strolled slowly across the fishmarket, like a man unobtrusively trying to use up time. Cora had spotted him on Torquato Accetto Bridge and grabbed the opportunity. She had been following her patient at a distance for well over a mile now. Half-heartedly. Her fear of discovery was so great she kept on dropping back and almost lost him, even though Nagy was going at such a gentle stroll a tortoise would have kept bumping into him. What was she to do with this trail that was leading nowhere? Clearly Nagy was just wandering aimlessly round the town. Now he was looking at the fish, brightly coloured fish in crushed ice. Bream, plaice, wolf-fish. Garnished with a few decoratively placed monkfish, special offer.

He seemed to have got hold of some money. He was wearing a new suit, white, and shoes that sparkled in the sun. It looked somehow wrong, like a disguise. Emphasised his greying temples.

Cora plucked up courage. What is it I'm afraid of?

The fishmarket was far enough away from Nagy's flat to make it look like a chance meeting. Definitely.

'Stanislaus!'

Nagy behaved as if he didn't know the woman and leant over the assortment of seafood, only turning round when she shouted his name out loud across the square. He gave her an exasperated look and made no move towards her. His greeting was, 'Why do you keep following me?'

'What? Me? You're being paranoid.'

'Did you seriously believe I wouldn't notice? I can feel your looks, like snails you've thrown at me. Sticking to me. Crawling up my back. What do you want?'

'I thought we were friends . . .'

How timid she sounded, despite all her good intentions.

'What do you want?'

'Nothing. What should I want? If you'd like to have another talk, we could . . .'

'What about?'

'Anything.'

'All that nostalgic stuff? God and the world? Leave me in peace.'

'And Maria?'

'What about Maria?'

'Have you told me everything?'

'Fuck off!'

He turned away abruptly, slipping between pedestrians as if they were slalom posts, and disappeared in the throng. Cora felt the blood rush to her cheeks. She was happy. If she'd meant nothing to him he would never have reacted in such an emotional way.

Tears came to her eyes. Not from happiness but her contact lenses.

As fragile as gold leaf, the sky arched over the town in thin layers, supported by a smog-reinforced red glow on one side, a storm front on the other.

In a boutique specialising in autumn fashions fraught with significance, Cora acquired a pair of blue suede gloves. They almost came up to her elbows.

The young blonde with the pony-tail had not been in the nude cleaning business long, as her embarrassed blushes clearly indicated. When offered a tax-free bonus to take up the spade and dig a grave, she forgot her supposed role and called the suggestion perverted, declaring garden work was not part of her job-description. What could have been a basis for negotiation was blown up into a matter of principle. Robert had no alternative but to inter the tomcats himself, then write his justified letter of complaint about such an inflexible employee to the management.

In the course of her observations Cora noted a certain regularity in Nagy's movements, which took him across the market and the harbour promenade between six and half past. Watching him from different hiding places, a cafe, for example, a viewpoint or various crowds, she was able to reconstruct his route section by section. In order to avoid confrontation, she only reconnoitred the point at which he disappeared from view on the morning of the following day. By these means she discovered his new place of work, the Alhambra. He was appearing there – it made her laugh out loud – as a magician.

There was a poster showing him in top hat and tails, black-and-white, grainy and less-than-life-size: *Let The Great Bagarozy* (sounded familiar from somewhere or other) *transport you into a world of illusion.* Underneath were colour pictures of go-go girls in minimal costume. Further posters advertised a snake-tamer by the name of Musetta and the high point of the evening's entertainment, a female impersonator, *The Divine Circe and Her Seven Little Pigs.*

Erika (15) says 'I do', then dies

Dallas: 15-year-old Erika Valdez, fatally ill with leukaemia, had only one wish: to get married before she died. The doctors had given her only a few weeks to live when she met good-looking college student, 19-year-old Joaquin Valdez, and fell in love with him. Erika, marked by chemotherapy, told her mother, 'I'm sure he doesn't like me, I look like a monster.' She was wrong. Joaquin returned her love and fulfilled her last wish, a white wedding. Erika went to the altar in a lace-trimmed wedding dress. After they exchanged vows the couple had only a few hours left before Erika died in her husband's arms. She was buried in her wedding dress.

Cora laughed all the way home. She couldn't stop laughing even when she was sitting across the table from Robert, eating her supper. At first he found her good humour threatening. What had been so funny in the practice? She was still laughing as she waved his question aside. Her strange behaviour reached its height when she handed him a newspaper cutting across the table, asking him if he could use it in his collection.

Robert was moved as he read the news item. Delighted, he blew a kiss to his wife. How radiant she looked! How young she looked without her glasses! Almost the same woman he had courted all those years ago. Well, there was undeniably a certain similarity.

'What have you been laughing at all the time?'
   'Oh . . . nothing . . . it's too pathetic.'

19

SUNDAY

The Alhambra was a music-hall-cum-nightclub with bilious green lighting, an old-style tourist trap with shows at the end of which the snake-charmer took off her tiger-skin leotard. Two drinks coupons included in the entrance fee. The psychedelic froth started in the cloakroom. The walls behind the two bars were covered with mirrors, the counters with chrome and hostesses, every smile a contribution to the company's save-as-you-earn scheme. Just waiting for a customer to invite them to his table. A whisky sour cost five drinks coupons. Pulsating fluorescent rings had been let into the dance floor, above it a revolving sphere covered in mirror-tiles flashed and glittered. Dance-hall music with a dogged beat. Then silence. Flourish on the drums. Cue for the MC, accompanied by a venerable, greybeard joke too decrepit to make it to the audience, even with the Zimmer frame of the MC's ingratiating smile. Flourish on the drums.

Top hat and tails, white gloves and stick: Nagy-Bagarozy looked great. But it all had a depressingly anachronistic elegance, like a travelling circus where the gouty elephant bellows with loneliness and the llama and pony beg for food outside the village supermarket. The kind of circus that only manages to survive because people think they owe it to their children.

He did the usual tricks with rings, handkerchiefs and mirrors. The trick with the floating woman. Nagy-Bagarozy didn't do it too badly. The young woman floated, apparently held up by the energy from his outstretched hands. She was good-looking and had hardly any clothes on. Her bodice flew open. The mixture of sex and magic went down well with the audience, was greeted with applause, wolf-whistles and proposals of marriage. Nagy 'carried' the woman from one end of the stage to the other, his left hand circling round under her buttocks. Then he saw Cora. And froze.

The woman fell to the floor like a stone, hurt herself and let out an oath. The audience went wild, delighted with the surprising variation. Nagy left the stage. The applause subsided to bewildered silence. The MC, somewhat baffled himself, asked the audience to bear with them – technical difficulties, you know – announced a change in the order of the programme and told his reserve joke. Cora took advantage of the confusion to slip backstage. Musetta, the snake-tamer, was just putting her python on.

'Where's Nagy?'

'Who?'

'Bagarozy.'

'Third door on the left.'

Cora felt for the light switch. Nagy wasn't there. A bare room, no windows or wallpaper. Dressing table, wooden chair. Cardboard boxes piled on top of each other. His white suit was hanging on the clothes stand in the corner. She ran to it, felt in every pocket, looking for papers. Her hand touched a metallic object. There was shouting in the corridor outside. Steps approaching. Cora folded her arms and stood there, prepared to give as good as she got.

Nagy seemed tense, but controlled. Tossed his top hat right past the tip of her nose into one of the cardboard boxes.

'You've just cost me my job.'

'Does a devil really need all this here?'

He gave a curt, hoarse laugh – 'If he wants to become human' – and performed the ritual of pulling off his gloves, finger by finger. Threw them into the wastepaper basket.

'What can I do for you?'

It sounded crude, as it was meant to. Cora went pale. The words struck deep.

'We haven't finished . . .'

'We haven't?' Nagy shrugged his neck and shoulders in a grotesque gesture, like a mime artist expressing cluelessness. 'Did I not put it politely? With great tact? Did I say you should go to the devil? On the contrary –'

'Maria's dead. I'm alive! Who have you got, if not me?'

'Who's dead and who's alive is often difficult to say

135

nowadays.' He edged round Cora in a semicircle of the largest possible radius as far as the dressing table and looked in the mirror. 'How can something that sings be dead? Something that stinks, yes. Something that becomes discoloured, certainly. Hmmm . . . you frighten me.' He lowered his voice. 'You're trying to outdo me. What do you want?' He held up a red velvet ball, closed his fist round it, opened out his fingers. 'Is that it?'

'No.'

Nagy asked Cora to look in her handbag. She obeyed, just to humour him, and found the ball between a tampon, the pistol and a condom. It took her by surprise, since Nagy had been at least three feet away from her all the time; on the other hand, people often did similar tricks on television which, she felt, entirely explained the phenomenon.

She threw the ball to him. He caught it and, as if he didn't quite know what to do with it, stuffed it in his ear.

'You still haven't told me the end of your story.'

'I haven't?'

'You know very well you haven't.'

Everything in his parallel world has to be great, colossal, tragic. He's ashamed because I've caught him doing his conjuror's act. I have to let him have his greatness. *Believe* him.

Nagy was in his vest and underpants. He took the white suit off its hanger.

'It's true, I haven't told you everything. What's the point?'

'To make it come true.'

She must have found the right tone of voice. His expression lost its smugness, became reflective. Through the walls came the booming bass of oriental music. Music to charm snakes by. How cold it was in here. Say something. Give me your world and take mine away from me. Never have I fallen so deeply in love, nor will I ever do so again. Buy my soul, throw it away, do what you like, but do it to me. I'd love to destroy you, I'd really love to destroy you. To help you become human.

Nagy looked into her eyes with a wistful, almost startled look.

'Come with me.'

Cora followed him down a long corridor and out of the rear entrance into the dark courtyard tight-parked with cars.

'Would you like to see my cellar?'
'Love to.'

In silence they walked past the pier where the amusement stalls had just closed down for the night. The railings were lined with night anglers and courting couples, staring at the water in unison. Rubbish bins were being loaded onto motor boats. Many of the fishing lines had phosphorescent floats. They looked pretty among the agitated stars.

'Have you shown this cellar to anyone before?'
'No.'

They crossed Accetto Bridge. It was chilly.

'Sorry about the job.'
'That's okay.'

Nagy's coat bellied out in the wind. He fiddled with something at his hip, pressed buttons, put small earphones in his ears and stopped for a moment, listening to the music the way people draw on their first cigarette after a long abstinence.

'Would you like . . . ?'

Cora smiled an 'I'd rather not', as if she were being offered drugs.

'Did you really kiss Tamara?'

To talk about that woman, he murmured, was to put the walk-on part centre stage. Didn't she think it would be better to say nothing for a while? Cora admitted he was right, even though the silence brought some absurd thoughts to the surface of her mind, even the idea, only an 'idea', of course, of offering him the vacant position of receptionist to tide him over until he found work. As part of a resocialisation programme on the job, as you might say. Italian psychiatrists had been practising it for years. Not as absurd as it might at first appear. She also felt the urge to tell him about her dream, or to ask him how the trick with his assistant landing on her backside worked. Temptations to break the silence with chatter which she managed to stifle.

With the silence and the change in surroundings came fear. Nagy cut through back lanes and alleyways which might well reduce the walk in real time, but made it *feel* as if it were taking a lot longer. He moved with the assurance of a sleepwalker, while she walked with arms outstretched, groping her way through the pitch darkness. As soon as his silhouette reappeared an obscure sense of security returned.

People of today
Seattle: Mitchell Rupe, a heavyweight American bank robber, is too heavy for the gallows. 41-year-old Rupe, who killed two bank clerks in 1981, was condemned to death by hanging. So far his considerable weight of 29 stones has kept him from the gallows. A court in Seattle found that, because of his weight, Rupe might be beheaded on the gallows, a form of execution which would violate the 'principle of human dignity'. At the moment discussions are being held as to whether Rupe should be hanged with a special rope or executed by injection. All along Rupe could have opted for injection, but has steadfastly refused. In the meantime the prisoner is stuffing himself with French fries and candy.

They reached the tower block. Nagy pointed to the stairs beside the lift that led down to the cellar.

'Are you ready?'
   'Yes.'

It was a long, U-shaped corridor, divided up on either side into cells separated by plywood walls and with metal grilles at the front. Anything more prosaic than this shared cellar space could hardly be imagined. Cora wished Nagy had taken her to some more theatrical setting, such as the pier or the park, which would have made it easier for her to put on a believable display of belief. He unlocked the last cell but one and switched on the light. The neon flicker in the corridor was reinforced by the dull yellow of a low-wattage bulb.

The cellar was roughly fifteen feet square. And empty. Empty, that is, apart from a few small objects. Photos, newspapers, cigarette packets in piles of varying heights. On the bare concrete. The bulkiest thing to meet the eye was a well-filled plastic bag and, on the wall at the back, at last!, a poster showing Maria with the soft lines and imploring eyes of a consumptive beauty.

'I haven't kept very much. Over the years most of the things became worthless. Bric-a-brac.'

Nagy switched on a halogen lamp suspended from two wooden battens, picked up the plastic bag and emptied the contents over the floor, stirring them round as if they were druidical paraphernalia. Photos and magazine articles, visiting cards and invitations, knick-knacks such as liqueur glasses, bows, medals, tubes of pills, coins, dice, a doll, a silk stocking, a marble . . . and other things whose nature and function were not obvious at a glance.

'When I first saw you, you reminded me of something.'
  'What?'
'Something horrible.'
'Oh, thank you very much.'
'Something that tormented me and yet made you attractive to me. Then, when you stopped wearing your spectacles and started going round on those ridiculous high heels, I didn't like it at all. You were refusing to remind me of it. Rebelling against it.'

What was it he was talking about, Cora wanted to know. The corridor light went out. With the reduced lighting, the cellar lost its prosaic air and turned into a meeting place for masked conspirators, or for anatomy students during theocentric times, whispering as they bent over their stolen corpse.

'I'm talking about horror. Do you know her last picture?' He pulled out something from the bottom of a pile. 'The old woman with me under her arm and carrying a plastic bag in the other hand. You just have to look at that picture, words are superfluous.'

Cora was speechless. This wasn't madness at all, this was an insult.

'Isn't the similarity striking?'

'You can't mean it seriously! Not even as a joke! I'm much younger than that woman. And I'm pretty. What's all this crap you're talking?'

'Please! Try to be objective. You keep getting hung up on minor details. Okay, delete the poodle and plastic bag, replace the horn-rims with a pair of gold spectacles . . .'

'What was it you wanted to tell me?'

So that's the way he saw me the whole time. As an old wreck of a woman.

'It was taken the day before Maria died. The last in a series of pictures which were necessary for her iconisation. What is an icon? Gossip and gossip columns. Reduction to a few pictures which, placed one over the other, reveal a monster. Imitations claiming to be essence. Do you understand? Can you imagine what it's like to live, breathe, walk around, be seen, only not for what you are, but for what you were and always *will be*? When people ignore your physical presence and seem to be talking to an image. A living image, brought to the surface by a daily sloughing of the skin. When her voice faded, so did her beauty. Maria the woman disappeared from view and already her monument was appearing through her skin. La Divina, idolised by millions, was lonely. She bought an apartment in Paris, where audiences had idolised her more than anywhere else. The apartment looked like . . . a mausoleum. As if the architect had been commissioned by the Légion d'honneur to create a dignified setting for an urn with very famous contents. It was all so cold. The Great Drawing Room with its Steinway grand and Renaissance pictures, the Red Drawing Room with its chinoiserie, the Louis Seize Dining Room, the Blue Room for all kinds of mementos: nothing looked lived in.

And in the bedroom stood the massive baroque Italian double bed from the time of her marriage to Meneghini. There was only one room in the whole apartment that seemed alive, that had character, and that was the bathroom, where Maria spent the larger part of the day. It was in white and pink marble, with gold taps, lots of mirrors, a couch and an armchair covered in orange velvet. Beside it, a telephone and a record player. A gaudy, sad refuge, like the private cabinet of a museum director. That's where she sat listening to old recordings, rang her friends. Friends? Contemporaries would be a better word.

It wasn't that she didn't go out and meet people. She gave masterclasses for talented young sopranos. When one of them made a poor attempt at some passage and Maria, to show how it would sound better, opened her mouth and what came out was not better, not even good, just shrill, tortured tones, like a punctured concertina – can you imagine? – it was hell. A hell I would have been proud of myself in the old days. And what was especially grim: greatness which has been destroyed is never *bad*, even in the extreme of destruction. Tragic, yes, terrible, certainly. But *mediocre*? Impossible!

'74, her last tour, in Japan like a washed-up footballer. It was coming close to mere noise. But then, in '76, she gave one final, private concert in Paris. It was . . . indescribable. Not musical notes any more but sawn-off screams. The music of damned souls, a cry of protest against everything. Accompanying herself on the piano, she sang Beethoven's 'Ah, perfido!' Without realising it, she meant *me*. Every note from her tattered vocal chords was aimed at me, pierced me.

All I wanted now was for Maria to die, for this torment, this unworthy existence to be brought to an end. First, though, the photograph had to be taken. It took quite a few attempts. And then, she was only fifty-three!' His voice choked, the tears were running down his cheeks. Cora did not feel sorry for him. He gradually calmed down. He spoke softly, as if in an ecstatic trance.

'That night I rang at the door of her apartment in the avenue Georges Mandel. She invited me in! That was how lonely she was! I introduced myself as the one I am. Immediately she screwed up her myopic eyes and her lips became thin and severe. She could smell me! I swear it's true! And still she invited me into her kitchen.

We had a long conversation. It lasted the whole night and all of the following morning. I told her everything, just as I've told you, my secret life at her side, every detail. At first, like you, she didn't believe me, but I had too much evidence, things no one else could know, jigsaw pieces that fitted into the puzzle that was her life. I spread out Maria's life before her, like a biography, let her see everything one more time, through my eyes. Do you remember, I said, that time in '58 in Rome when you had to break off Norma half way through because you'd lost your voice? The mob wanted to lynch you and groups of people stood outside your hotel until five in the morning, chanting 'Die, Maria, die'? During that night you clung onto Toy, wondering whether you could carry on. And you said to yourself, if he barks three times, everything'll be all right. I barked three times. I was lying.

And I told her about the beach on Skorpios, Onassis's island, where I once bit a snake to death and laid it at her feet. She hated snakes. She never told anyone about it, she had this superstition it would be unlucky to talk about it. She gave a scream of revulsion and buried the blood-covered viper with sand. It was part of me. I also told her about beautiful, very private episodes. And I fooled her into believing Onassis's last word before being wheeled into the oxygen tent was 'Maria'. Sometimes she laughed, sometimes she bit her lip or stared, wide-eyed, at all this deception. Then, late in the night, she asked me whether she should sing Traviata again. *Sing Traviata again!*

She still believed her voice had just gone on holiday and would be coming back some time! I said, Don't do it, there's no point. And she looked at me, and whispered Aida's words, *Tutta e finita sulla terra per noi?* And I, her Radames, replied, *E vero.* Above us played music of the last things, and it was true, everything was over on earth for us. Something like the wing-beat of a bird bigger than the sun and the moon passed across the sky. Ten thousand parachute stars fell on Paris. He looked upwards, a beatific smile on his face.

'Suddenly we weren't in a kitchen any longer, not sitting at a table. The walls and ceiling disappeared. Before us was an ocean, dark, streaked with the first, hesitant grey of dawn. The sand we were sitting on was from hour-glasses that had stopped. In the haze of the far distance the sea was edged with a razor-sharp blade of light. Slowly it approached us, a torpedo from the silver zone, dividing the sea and the sky for the coming day. It glided, flew through the water, creating waves and foam, shipwrecks and rocks. We sat for a long time, staring out to sea, in silence. Indescribable silence. As I had done so often before, I looked at her hands and arms. She had very beautiful, slender hands, hands which could transform mere roles into rounded characters, hands that had no difficulty expressing any emotion, whose gestures and movements never seemed exaggerated, never came at the wrong time. Then, I'll never forget it, she stroked my chin. Tenderly, forgivingly, she touched me. ME. The first time. What I had been hoping for for decades. She said nothing, just touched my chin, stood up, in her gigantic majesty, got into the bath, it was midday, and died. Out of her dead body came a marble foetus. The rest was cremated and the ashes scattered over the Aegean.' By this time Nagy's voice was almost inaudible. He had sat down and clamped his head between his knees.

'I sat in silence at the water's edge for days on end. I felt as if with Maria's death two things, which belonged together since the very beginning of the cosmos, had become one. My memory bore me away, along a flight-path of amber and gold, far back to the time when I still had wings. Beautiful wings . . . But why am I telling you all this? Most of the money went to her mother. Dotting the i and crossing the t in tragic. It all fitted together, perfectly.' He looked up and grinned.

'I couldn't die like Maria, just because it was all over with me. I clung on to myself, a memento of my own past. I spent twenty years creeping round a world which wasn't my world any longer. Finally I went to you. Now you know.'

He gave Cora a searching look. 'And don't believe it.'

'But I do.'

'Lying only makes you more unbearable. And I had such high hopes of you.'

'I believe everything you say.' She took his arms.

'Don't touch!'

'You kissed that stupid cow, Tamara, and I can't even touch you?'

'There's a difference between kissing and touching. You want a kiss? Okay.'

Cora shrank back. His eyes had narrowed to slits.

'You wouldn't harm me?'

'You do so much to harm yourself, what need is there of me?'

He seized her by the shoulders, pulled her to him and kissed her. Cora felt some hot, alien thing push its way into her mouth and swell up in her throat, threatening to suffocate her. Her gorge rose and with both hands she pushed Nagy away from her, gasping for breath.

'Satisfied?' He wiped his lips with the back of his hand. 'You were the most miserable piece of shit in human form I could find. You could have saved me. Now at least save me from *you*. What concern of *yours* is Maria?'

'Don't talk like that.'

'And if it were the case that I'm crazy, that there's a world inside me which isn't like yours; if it were the case that everything around was crying out IT ISN'T TRUE! YOU'RE SICK, WE'RE THE HEALTHY ONES, where would be the attraction in your healthiness? Where would its beauty lie? Once the earth was one big party for me, a ballroom, infinite scope, a nocturnal department store. And now? We're black and white comic-strip heroes. Clichés tumbling from one ear to the next through a vast, grey void. I haven't discovered anything worth coming back to in your land. You're nothing but a noisy, lumbering mixture of decomposition gases! To say you're alive's a euphemism of the first order.

There was so much you could have done to make something of yourself, so much. It's all purely academic now, or material for a hired Hollywood hack for whom no happy end can be too far-fetched, providing the money's good. Your body's a mass grave of wasted opportunities and stifled dreams, impossible to approach without an oxygen mask, and even then it makes one want to puke!'

Cora's mouth was a pale thin line. Fists clenched, white-knuckled, she desperately searched for some word that would adequately express her fury.

'Devil?' Nagy suggested, gallant as ever.

'You swine! You miserable, poxy swine!'

Nagy pouted his lips in a malicious mockery of hurt feelings, popped the headphones of his Walkman in his ears and just stood there, silent, until she ran off.

20

SCORCHED EARTH

September had been a reprise of the summer. Perhaps that was the reason why October felt obliged to catch people out with some early night frosts. The carnivorous plants Cora had bought as a weapon in her fight against fruit flies and then, disappointed with the results, put out in the garden were no match for them and were butchered en masse. The moment Robert saw the plants lying there, all limp and lifeless, he felt sorry for them and chucked them on the compost heap, still in their terracotta pots. It seemed cruel to tear these tropical victims of the northern climate out of the homes that had become their coffins. This led him, as so often – as most of the time actually – to reflect on the fact that all flesh-eating plants are as grass, so that he only noticed the salesmanlike figure after it had already negotiated the garden gate and was holding out its hand in an offer of mutual acquaintance which Robert, given his upbringing, found himself incapable of refusing.

It was odd that the stranger with the vacant, slightly tortured expression of the sales endomorph neither announced his name nor tacked any explanation onto his suggestion that they had better sit down, there were things to discuss. Pondering this and formulating a protest in his mind, Robert watched as the man took possession of a wicker chair and began to spread papers from his briefcase out over the glass top of the table.

'We're insured for everything.'

Robert thought that should take the wind out of his visitor's sails.

Entirely unmoved, without even a covert reaction to Robert's statement, the intruder continued to pull out sheets of paper, lists, then drew his fountain pen and peered up at Robert with a strange look. Some of the papers were covered in tiny, illegible writing.

'We have to talk about your death.'

'I'm sorry?'

'You heard me alright. Because of the frequent complaints about our mode of operation, which people often claim is abrupt, or disgusting, or difficult to understand . . .' – the man snorted and dabbed the sweat from his forehead with the tips of his fingers – ' . . . we have decided to make an experiment, to try out what you might call a new strategy. We want to get the subject more closely involved at the planning stage in the manner and time of his decease . . .'

'The subject?'

'You, in this case.'

'Leave my house this moment!'

'Come now . . . why not cooperate . . . Otherwise you'll only end up losing your temper.'

'I . . . I . . .'

'You're a collector yourself, aren't you? That's excellent. I've brought along a few ideas of our own.'

'This is . . . in the very worst possible taste! Appalling!'

'If you say so, sir. Here we have a car accident, next week. Somewhat short notice, I agree, but it would all be over very quickly, at top speed, literally. Almost completely painless.'

'I don't drive!'

'But the other man does. Our second offer: a heart attack in two years time. Not a quick death; paralysed for several days; great pain. What you've always been afraid of.'

Robert didn't answer, having decided it must be a nasty practical joke on the part of some of his colleagues.

'Thirdly, oh, but this is spectacular, really spectacular, satanists drugged out of their skulls break into your house and torture you for hours until you die. Your wife as well.'

'In how many years would that be?'

'Five . . .'

'That's something, at least.'

'Take your time over it. Of course, the moment after you have come to your decision, you'll have forgotten it. We're not sadists.'

'Will I be born again?'

'You? What for? Well, possibly, but that's not our

department. And – Oh, there's something else here . . . Hmm, passing away peacefully at ninety-four . . .'

'I'll take that.'

The stranger grinned and lowered his eyes. 'Only a joke. You must excuse me. Do you never offer anyone a drink? Ah well, let's get this tied up. What do you think?'

At that moment Robert woke up, bathed in sweat. The bedroom light had been switched on. He saw his wife standing beside the bed and gave a groan of relief because it had only been a dream. Cora was wearing long suede gloves. She aimed Nagy's revolver at her husband and pressed the trigger.

Robert's last thought was, it could have been much . . .

21

Cora threw the gun into a hedge, close to the house where it was sure to be found. Then she walked to her practice, burnt the gloves and transcript and rang the police. A patient, she said, who was obsessed with her, had threatened to kill her husband, and he wasn't answering the phone, couldn't they send a patrol car round to check up, she was very worried . . . things started moving in the direction Cora wanted them to move.

Local news: 41-year-old Robert D. was murdered last night in his own home. According to the police, the murderer must have climbed over the garage roof to gain access to the bedroom, where he fired three shots at close range. The prime suspect is a patient of the dead man's wife, Cora D., a 37-year-old psychiatrist. The presumed motive was jealousy. It is also a possibility that the patient, who is mentally disturbed, wanted to provide proof of his claim he is the Devil in person.

Cora had no problems with the interrogation next morning. No one had any reason to doubt her version of events. Lioba Rosenbaum, brought in as psychological consultant, blamed herself, and, overcome with genuine remorse, could hardly look her former fellow student in the face.

The detective leading the murder enquiry told her they had broken into the suspect's apartment but had not found him there, only his dog, and even that had managed to escape.

Cora shook her head weakly. 'He hasn't got a dog . . .'

'He certainly has. And what a dog! Absolutely refused to let itself get caught. It was fantastic: the poodle dashes past us into the lift, jumps up and presses the ground-floor button with its nose. Since then neither hide nor hair of it has been seen. Incredible, don't you think.'

Cora, suddenly tormented by hot flushes, wanted to be alone and asked if she might leave the station, permission for which was granted. At the door she turned round:

'Did you look in the freezer?'

'We certainly did! Do you know what was in it?'

'No . . .'

'Its predecessor!'

'What do you mean, its predecessor?'

'The dog's.'

'Sorry?'

'A white poodle, frozen solid. I know people sometimes like to keep funny things, but that . . .'

WEEK 22

Cora's deed was without consequences, either good or bad. Unpunished, unhappy, she spent every day out in the streets, walking round the city in search of Nagy. If the police couldn't find him, how could she? Still, there was nothing left for her to do but to search for him. She had given up her practice and was living off Robert's insurance. It wasn't enough for a house in the hills, but she didn't care, she didn't care about anything while Nagy was nowhere to be found. At night she left the ground-floor doors open, dreaming that Nagy would come and hide in her house, take his revenge on her, stab, throttle or beat her to death. Anything as long as he was there.

It was months later, when her hopes had almost faded, that she saw him, one afternoon, while she was standing at the end of the harbour wall, where saltwater and freshwater mingled, chains and seaweed-encrusted ropes hung down. In a long black coat with the collar turned up, he was leaning against the wall of a building alternately watching the ducks on the narrow embankment and three men grouped round a thimblerigger. They didn't even bother to try to involve him in the game. He was unshaven, his hair greasy, his coat old and filthy.

A barge came bobbing past. On the roofing felt over the cabin sat a little girl who was alternately waving and thumbing her nose at everyone. She was touching, without being aware of it. She looked like the doll in Nagy's drawer. It could be her imagination, of course. Or coincidence. What was it Robert used to say? Coincidence is capable of anything.

The girl was very pretty and very grubby. Nagy watched her glide past, his expression unmoved, and as he did so, his glance naturally fell on Cora. It didn't stop, but continued following the girl into the city, along under the February trees, towards the skyscrapers.